THE GIRL TRIUMPHANT

THE GIRL TRIUMPHANT

THE LAST VAMPIRE™ BOOK 8

JUDITH BERENS   MARTHA CARR   MICHAEL ANDERLE

LMBPN Publishing
PMB 196, 2540 South Maryland Pkwy
Las Vegas, NV 89109

First US edition, November 2019
eBook ISBN: 978-1-64202-598-9
Print ISBN: 978-1-64202-599-6

DEDICATIONS

From Martha

To everyone who still believes in magic
and all the possibilities that holds.
To all the readers who make this
entire ride so much fun.
And to my son, Louie and so many wonderful friends who
remind me all the time of what
really matters and how wonderful
life can be in any given moment.

From Michael

To Family, Friends and
Those Who Love
To Read.
May We All Enjoy Grace
To Live The Life We Are
Called.

CHAPTER ONE

It didn't take more than a few seconds for Jim Trembo's life to be at risk. Even in the dim light of the candles burning in the basement of the old Austrian church, he could see the glint of knives held out in front of some of the black-robe-clad members of the Circle.

They couldn't see the smile on his face.

That was a lot faster than I was expecting. I figured I could get a few words in first, but I guess I'd better talk fast.

He held his palms out in case any of them could see. "My friends, I come in peace and unity with your cause. Please, hear me out."

A deep, gravelly voice boomed from the far side of the group. "You are trespassing on sacred ground. You have interrupted holy work."

"No, no. I wish to be a *part* of this work." He stepped forward slowly. "I have come from America, and I sympathize with what you do."

"You do not know what we do." The booming voice

showed caution in his tone. "Our work is kept from the public."

"Well, that's not exactly true." Jim smirked. "I found you guys online. Whether you intended it or not, somebody has made your work very public."

One of the knives moved closer, raised by invisible hands to eye level only a few feet away from the trespasser.

"Hold," the voice said. "Let him speak. So, you know what we do. Why are you here?"

Jim carefully lowered his hands and straightened his shirt, which had shifted awkwardly in the commotion. *Get flowery. Match them. It's the only way they'll trust you.* "I have been drawn here. It is almost as though I was sent here. It was destiny that we meet. You see, I have been in the presence of an evil force, one you claim to fight with your very existence."

"A vampire," the voice growled.

Jim's smile grew wider. "A vampire, yes. There is a vampire in the United States of America." He shuffled his feet and moved slightly closer after he saw the knives lowered. "The vampire is young, female, and dangerous. I believe I can remove her from the world we live in." *Man, who talks like this?* "But I need your help."

"We are not a trusting group," the voice replied. "We keep to ourselves. Our work is passed down through the generations. The Circle has never been broken. It is only for those in the bloodline. Just because one of us falls, it does not mean we must go outside the bloodline. Everyone here belongs to that bloodline except you."

Sensing hostility in his voice. I better close this deal or they're going to cut me to pieces. "Today, I do not ask to be a part of your group. I understand the sanctity of it. All I am asking is for help. If we work together, we can finally make the vampire race extinct."

A murmur rumbled through the group of cloaked men. A few of them slipped their knives back into their sheaths.

Forget about making her extinct, though. I'm going to make her a weapon of war that nobody can stop.

"What is your name?"

"Trembo. Jim Trembo. I work for the federal government of the United States of America."

Immediately upon hearing that, the group drew their knives again.

Jim expected it that time. "Hang on, hang on. It's okay. I am not here on official business. Any details I see or receive here will be kept to myself. I will not share your secrets with anyone else in the world. I promise."

"Why should we trust you?"

Ugh. Can we just get this over with? "Because I found you. How many people have interrupted your meetings before?"

"No one."

"And how long have you been having meetings?"

"We have met in this crypt for more than five centuries."

"Exactly. I was compelled by a higher power to find you, board a plane, fly across the ocean, and descend these stairs in this church to be in your presence. Does that not prove the existence of a higher power leading me to you?" Nobody responded. The air felt like a vacuum. "I don't wish to interrupt your work. I just wish to help it along. I can capture the girl. I have your sword in my possession."

From under his hood, the man with the deep voice widened his eyes. "You have our sword?"

"Sure. Not here. It's back home. But I have it, and I know what power it wields. The reason I am here is that I just need guidance on where to go. Who is this girl? What's her name?"

"Why would we tell you? Who says we know that information?"

"Because your sword was found in the middle of a field with the blood of the girl on the soil. You guys already have these answers because the three who went before you found her just fine. Now it's my turn, and I can use the sword, too."

But the group wasn't having it. "Leave. This is not your job; it is ours. We will find a way, even if it means forging a new sword and blessing it ourselves."

Jim ran his fingers through his hair, steadying himself because he knew it was about to get a little more interesting. "I'm not leaving."

"What? You dare to disobey the sacred orders of The Circle?"

"Yeah, pretty much." Jim shrugged. "You're going to talk to me today. You're going to give me the information I need, and then I will leave you alone to your little meeting here."

"I sense insolence in your tone," the voice snarled.

"I should hope so. I'm a hundred percent insolent right now. You guys are going to tell me who this girl is. I spent nearly an entire day traveling to get here. Just give me her name, and I'll go."

"This is your last warning, Mr. Trembo." The knives

were raised again. "If you do not remove yourself from these premises, there will be dire consequences."

Jim folded his arms across his chest. "Don't threaten me. I'm here to help you."

The man shook his head. "No, you're not. You are here for yourself. You do not wish to fulfill our prophecies or assist us in our mission. You are here for selfish reasons. I can sense that."

Two of the men charged at Jim and pressed him against the stone wall. The back of his head smacked the rock, and he grunted on impact. A lump swelled on his scalp, and the cold steel of a knife blade pressed against his throat. He lifted his chin, trying to keep still.

"Do not struggle." The man with the booming voice walked toward him. The group parted to let him through. "Right now, you stand among those who took an oath of silence. You breathe the same air that holds the dead. This crypt is the final resting place of many saints. With one move, you can join them, and nobody will know."

Jim tried to pull his arms free, but the men held him tighter, squeezing his arms and slamming them against the wall. "Real honorable, guys, ganging up...what, three on one?"

"Honor in a man's eyes is different than true honor."

"What the heck does that mean?"

"What you see as 'honorable' and 'dishonorable' is subjective, and we work from our divine orders. We live our lives by those orders, and preventing you from interfering in our mission is the highest honor we can aspire to."

This guy talks like a fortune cookie. "Sir, I know it looks like you are in control here, but I promise you, you're not. You better let me go now so we can all talk this over like adults. Otherwise, you're going to regret it."

The blade pressed harder against his throat. Any movement and it would break the skin.

"You know too much. You are not permitted to know any more. It is time to meet your Maker and answer to your sins."

Okay, you asked for it. Jim kicked the knife-wielder in the stomach, causing him to drop the blade. A skirmish broke out in response. Because the two men holding him were distracted, he pulled his arms loose and punched each of them in the face, swinging wildly.

"You dare to…" The booming voice was cut off by a stiff jab to the face from Jim.

Should've kept your mouth shut. All you did was make it easier for me to find you. Jim wrapped his arm around the man's neck, wrenching it tightly. He reached around his back and pulled out a gun, which he held to the man's temple. He cocked the hammer, and the click froze everyone in their tracks.

"See, that's what I figured." Jim tightened his arm on the man's neck while keeping the barrel of the gun pressed to the side of his head. "Don't say I didn't warn you. You guys brought knives to a gunfight. You didn't have a chance. Should've listened."

The man remained still, as did everyone around him, and cautioned, "Nobody moves forward. Let the intruder speak."

"Funny how quickly things change, hey?" Jim pushed the gun harder into his skull. "I'm a pretty good shot, and this thing has plenty of bullets in it. I can kill you now, then start mowing down the rest of you before any of you realize what is going on. This isn't a time for any of you to be a hero. Instead, we're all going to work together. Got it?"

"Threats of death will not work with us." The voice remained defiant. "Our mission will live on, and we will reap the rewards our brothers who were cut down during their pilgrimage to America are currently enjoying."

"Yeah, yeah, whatever. Here's the deal: I pull this trigger once, and not only do you die, but there are people upstairs right now in silent worship. You think they won't hear this? You'll all be exposed, whoever survives. Your mission will be over, and it won't live on. That vampire girl *will* live on, and she will breed. The world will be filled with vampires, and everything you've worked for over the past centuries will be unraveled. Then what? Your stubbornness will cause your downfall."

The man stopped resisting since what Jim said was true. "I cannot argue that point, but you are treading on dangerous ground."

"Uh-huh. Doesn't matter. If I don't get my hands on this vampire girl, just like you, my life will have been worth nothing. I have nothing to lose. Even if somehow you overpower me and seal me into a crypt down here? I'm not afraid of it. If I can't remove that vampire from American society, I might as well die down here, alone. But instead of leaving this holy building full of the bodies of men who accomplished nothing with their lives, maybe you can just tell me the name of the girl who killed your men. Then I can walk away peacefully, and you can rest secure in the knowledge that your vampire problem is being taken care of by someone who knows what he's doing."

"We don't know her name."

"Liars."

"No, no! We do not lie, but we know who does have her name. The man who had the vision that led our brothers to America in the first place. If we send you to him, will you leave in peace?"

CHAPTER TWO

Vickie's hands trembled as she dipped the butter knife into the jar of peanut butter.

She hadn't stopped eating for hours. Her stomach was still rumbling, so she hoped a sandwich would finally satiate her. But as she scooped out more peanut butter, her fingers squeezed involuntarily, bending the metal knife until it was shaped like a *V*.

Frustrated, she tossed the knife on the counter, where it bounced off two other V-shaped butter knives.

Vickie fell forward, resting her elbows on the counter and holding her head in her hands. She took deep breaths to try to calm herself.

Come on. You're never going to be able to function if you can't get this under control. "Alexis?" she shouted as she closed her eyes.

"Yeah?" Alexis called from the back of the house.

"Can you come in here, please?"

Alexis emerged from the hallway and stopped in front

of her. "Yikes. You know peanut butter's not that hard to spread, right?"

"Shut up."

"I'm kidding." She placed her hand on Vickie's shoulder. "I thought you said you were feeling better?"

Vickie stood up straight, stretching out her back and trying to calm down her stomach pains. "You saw the look in Eric's eyes, didn't you?"

Alexis nodded as she scooped up the bent knives. "Oh, yeah. Like he was ready to have a heart attack. I think he thought you were going to keel over dead right there."

"Exactly. I wanted him to be okay, you know? It's bad enough that he knows everything. I didn't want him to feel like…" Her voice trailed off.

Alexis dumped the knives into the garbage can and closed the lid. "Like his wonderful, gorgeous girlfriend who he's madly in love with is trying to duck a bunch of people who want her dead?"

"Basically, yeah."

"I know." She pulled another butter knife from the drawer. "Here, let me make this for you before we have to go to the store and buy a new set of silverware." She scooped out some peanut butter and began spreading it on the piece of bread sitting on the plate. "So anyway, you lied to him."

"I didn't *lie*. I just thought I could get it under control like I always do. But I can't shake the feeling that something bad is happening. Something really, unbelievably dangerous to me personally."

Alexis stuck the knife back into the peanut butter and

turned to face her. "Do you think you're going to die? Is that what your sense is telling you?"

Vickie leaned against the refrigerator door. "I don't know what it's telling me. I'm in danger. Maybe it's death, maybe it's something worse. I don't know what would be worse than death, though."

"There are plenty of things worse than death." Alexis resisted the urge to talk about torture, figuring it wasn't the time or the place. "Are you able to get the jelly out of the fridge without shattering the jar?"

"I'll try." Vickie opened the fridge and pulled the jar out. The gelatinous purple goo on the inside of the jar jiggled as she handed it to Alexis. "There. I've been able to do *something*."

"Wow, those shakes are bad."

"It's all I can do to not go crazy. What am I supposed to do? I can't just be like this forever."

Alexis grabbed a spoon and scooped some jelly from the jar, dropping it onto a second piece of bread. "Can your sense tell you timetables? Like, if there's a threat coming, do you know how close it is?"

Vickie shook her head. "Not really. If it's an emergency, my instincts react, like that kid who fell into the creek or the dog at the intersection. But this kind of thing just gets worse when it gets closer. I can't tell how long it'll be."

"Hmm." Alexis flopped the two pieces of bread together and picked up the plate. "Sit down at the table. I'll carry this over. Now that I made one, I want one, too."

Minutes later, the two girls sat at the table, munching on peanut-butter-and-jelly sandwiches.

"Thanks for the help." Vickie chewed. "My instincts won't calm down, so my hunger is through the roof."

"Well, you're not wasting away to nothing. You're just burning a lot of energy with all this worry. We need to keep it together."

"I thought we *did* have it together."

Craig walked into the kitchen. "Sandwiches? At the kitchen table like civilized people? Whose house did I walk into? You two don't even have your phones out."

His daughter nodded at Vickie. "Somebody is still struggling."

Craig's amused expression fell. "Still? I thought you were feeling better."

"She just said that to make Eric feel better." Alexis chomped on her sandwich.

"Am I allowed to talk?" Vickie snapped.

"Sorry. Just trying to help."

"I didn't want Eric to worry. I feel like he has enough on his mind, dating a vampire and all."

Craig took a seat at the table. "And your senses are still all over the place?"

Alexis smirked. "You should check the garbage."

He looked at the garbage can, then back at Vickie. "Why?"

"I owe you a few butter knives." Vickie cracked a half-smile. "Sorry."

Craig waved his hand. "Forget the knives. You don't know how long this is going to last, do you?"

"Nope. It might last until I'm faced with whatever threat is out there, or maybe they'll take a break, and I'll feel all right. I don't know what I'm sensing right now. It's just bad."

"We need to find a way to keep it together. You can't hide from the rest of the world in the meantime."

"He's right," Alexis chimed in. "Stay home from work, and you lose your job. Stay home from school, and you'll fail out. Exams are coming up. We'll have more flexibility once we reach summer, but we have to get there first."

Craig grabbed Vickie's arm. "Can you concentrate? Can you think clearly?"

Vickie tilted her head back and forth as if she were shifting her brain around to see how loose it felt. "I feel okay, like I can think. I just have these spasms where I lose control of my powers and can't hide them. That's how the knives wound up in the garbage."

"Okay." Craig leaned back in his chair. "Theoretically, we can get through exams, then. If you can think clearly, you can still take them. Then we can get to summer and deal with it from there."

There was a beat of silence while Craig stared out the window and the girls continued eating their sandwiches. Vickie stared at her plate. "What if we don't make it to summer?"

"Are you worried this is all going down before then?" Alexis put her sandwich down. "Like, you think it's going to happen tomorrow, whatever it is?"

Vickie put her sandwich down too and licked a dollop of peanut butter off her thumb. "I don't know that I would say that. It might not be tomorrow, but do I have to live like this for weeks or months before it happens? And if it happens, and it's as bad as I feel it will be, am I going to die? What difference does it make to pass final exams if someone is going to cut off my head or whatever?"

Craig and Alexis exchanged concerned glances.

"We just need to find a way to function right now." Craig felt like he was giving a pep talk to Alexis about her mother's cancer. "We'll take it a day at a time. We can't live our lives worried about what might happen. All we can do is react to what is happening. We'll cross that bridge when we get there. In the meantime, let's focus our energy on staying as normal as possible."

"Whatever *that* looks like." Alexis chuckled. "Hard to be normal when your vampire sister is terrified that she's about to be beheaded."

"I don't know if I can be normal anymore. What does being a vampire mean if I'm hiding my powers all the time? Everything about me comes from my powers. I've struggled to keep them under wraps when I'm not at risk. How am I supposed to deal when I feel a grave danger creeping up on me?"

Craig tilted his head. "What you said would be true if you were just a vampire, but you're not. You're a member of this family. That's what makes you who you are. You're not hiding your powers because you're ashamed of your heritage. You're doing it for the safety and wellbeing of yourself and those around you. That's more powerful than the ability to run super-fast or whatever."

Vickie sighed. "I wish I could believe you. I understand what you are saying, but I am having a hard time existing right now."

"I know. We're here for you. Let's just work on staying as calm as possible. Meditate or something. You want to go run the field at night and get it out of your system there? Fine. Do what you need to do, as long as you are *sure* you are protected from being seen. I want you to have a healthy outlet, but I also don't want you to take unnecessary risks."

"Meanwhile, I'll be the sandwich maker around here." Alexis winked at her.

Vickie giggled. "Thanks, guys. I don't know how this is going to go, but I'm glad you're in my corner. I'm going to go lie down and see if I can rest."

"Good idea." Craig nodded.

"Leave the dishes. I got 'em." Alexis reached across the table and slid the plate toward her. After Vickie closed her bedroom door, Alexis looked at her father. "You think she can manage?"

"I don't know. I've struggled to figure out how vampires operate in the last year. I guess we'll find out."

"I feel so helpless. Like, I can make her sandwiches, but I want her to feel better too. She shouldn't have to suffer so much. She's not *doing* anything."

Craig smiled. "That's how I felt about your mom when she was going through chemo. Your mom wouldn't harm a fly, yet she went through all of this suffering. It seemed so unfair at the time. It *still* seems unfair when I think about it, but that's life. None of it is fair, and it often dumps on the innocent people."

Alexis pursed her lips. "I just hope Vickie's story has a happier ending than Mom's."

Craig thought of his supernatural interaction with his wife, when she assured him that she was okay. "I don't think your mom's story ended sadly for her. For us, it was a sorrowful chapter, but she's happy now. I know she is. And it's not over yet. Neither is Vickie's story."

"How do you deal with this helpless feeling?"

Craig stood up. "Well, I dealt with it by crying uncontrollably in private. But when you're with her, you just support her, help her, and do the best you can. You're already doing that."

"By making sandwiches?"

"Sometimes the simplest actions mean the most. You didn't make her a sandwich, you gave her a meal she couldn't put together on her own. She wouldn't be lying down if it wasn't for you. Small gestures have a big impact."

"I just want her to be okay."

"She will. Those are *my* instincts talking now."

CHAPTER THREE

Jim Trembo glanced at the dreary gray clouds overhead as he stepped off the bus. *Amazing how quickly you can get answers when you have the right tools.* He patted his chest, feeling the bulge of his gun poking out of its holster.

The previous night, he'd thought the Circle had given him all the information they could, but as he made his way up the sidewalk while raindrops bounced off his shoulders into the puddles at his feet, Jim had his doubts.

What if they are a bunch of liars? What if they sent me on this wild goose chase so I would put my gun away and they could scamper off? Why did I take their word for it?

He stood in front of the house, matching the address jotted on the slip of paper in his pocket. The petals of the pink and red flowers sprouting from the planters hanging off the windowsills bounced and danced as the rain hit them.

Even if they lied to me, what's my Plan B? Kill them, and still have nothing? The last thing I can do is to go home empty-

handed. I need information about this girl, and this is the only place to get it at this point.

A light rumble of thunder echoed through the sky, and the sprinkle of rain turned into a light drizzle. He pulled the collar of his coat up over the back of his neck, shivered, and walked up the short walkway to the front door of the quaint old house.

Jim knocked and took a polite step back to wait for an answer. He peered down the street. *Every house on this block is two stories except this one. I wonder why?*

"*Ich komme,*" a soft female voice called from inside. Jim pulled his hands out of his pockets and folded them in front of his body, trying not to look as though he was ready to pull a gun, even though he was.

The door opened up to a gray-haired, plain-faced woman with a pleasant, inviting smile. Her eyes squinted as her cheeks raised. "*Womit kann ich Ihnen behilflich sein?*"

Jim stumbled over his words, not expecting an old woman to greet him. "Um, yes, hi. Uh, *sprichst du Englisch?*"

The woman shook her head disappointingly. "*Nein, ich kann nicht. Vielleicht kann ich dir noch helfen?*"

Great. She doesn't speak English. "Does...does Simon live here? Simon?"

"*Ja, Simon wohnt hier. Möchten Sie mit ihm sprechen?*"

Jim shrugged and nodded, laughing awkwardly at his inability to speak German. She held up a finger to tell him to wait, then turned and shouted for Simon. She waved him into the front room of the house and pointed to a small upholstered chair. "*Bitte kommen Sie herein. Simon will bald hier sein.*"

Seems like she's getting Simon in here. "*Danke.*"

She smiled and bowed her head. *"Bitte."* The woman disappeared down the hallway.

Jim once again patted his chest to make sure his gun was there, just in case, but the tension melted when he saw Simon.

The man was old and decrepit. In fact, Jim heard Simon coughing and hacking as he shuffled down the hall to him. By the time he reached the front room, Simon had worked up whatever he had been coughing and smacked his lips together.

He had a permanent slouch, his spine curved as though he bore the weight of the world on his shoulders. His dark wood cane clunked against the furniture as he stepped onto the area rug sprawled across the middle of the room.

Simon extended his hand to Jim. *"Meine Haushälterin sagt, Sie wollten mit mir sprechen. Ich heisse Simon. Um was geht es hierbei?"*

Jim began waving his hands to stop him. "I'm sorry, sir, I don't speak German."

Simon snorted. "Oh, okay. Sorry." He groaned as he fell into the armchair across from Jim. "That woman is my housekeeper. Only speaks German. I speak both. She says you were looking for me."

Jim sat up onto the edge of his chair. "Yes, sir, I…" He was interrupted by another fit of violent coughing by the old man, who pulled out a handkerchief and held it to his mouth, dabbing his lips once he regained his breath. "The Circle sent me."

The man's lips parted. For a moment, it appeared to Jim as though he hadn't heard him, but he could see surprise in his eyes. "Excuse me."

He hoisted himself back up again and shuffled down the hallway to bark at his housekeeper.

"*Du musst für mich in den Laden gehen.*"

"*Jetzt?*"

"*Ja.*"

"*Was brauchst du?*"

"Gehen Sie einkaufen fur die Liste auf dem Kuhlschrank, sofort."

"*Was auch immer du sagst, Simon. Ich werde gleich zurück sein.*"

The footsteps again echoed through the house, and Jim heard the back door open and shut as Simon entered the room again and slowly sat down. "I just sent her to the store, so we can have some privacy here. I didn't want her hearing anything we had to say."

"What's the big deal? She doesn't speak English anyway."

"Son, you can't be too careful with this kind of information. What are you doing with the Circle?"

Jim crossed his legs, settling into a more comfortable position, knowing he was alone with the old man. "I'm… working with them. We have some things we are hashing out together. I met with them last night, and they assured me you were the man to speak to."

Simon cleared his throat. "I'm nothing special. I'm just a man who once attended the gatherings of the Circle, and now I don't. That's all."

"They called you a prophet."

He laughed. "Oh, did they? Well, they don't know what they're talking about. I'm no prophet. I only had a dream."

"A dream?"

"Yeah." He leaned his cane on the chair next to him. "I saw the girl. She showed up as clear as day in a vision. I don't think that makes me a prophet. It just means somebody at a higher pay grade than me decided I should see her. I reported it to the Circle, and they did the searching. I planted the seed, but that's about it."

"They wouldn't have gone after her if you hadn't seen her in your vision?"

"They didn't even know she existed." He shook his head disgustedly. "I was the one who opened up the whole thing. All they had to do was listen to me, and they had the rest of the information."

"Why weren't you at the meeting last night?" Jim leaned forward. "There were a lot of men there. You weren't among them, as far as I could tell."

"Have you looked at me? I can barely get up to go to the bathroom. Making it across town and down the steps of an old church is beyond my body's abilities now. Besides, I have had disagreements with the group as a whole."

"You didn't support their mission?"

Simon scowled at him. "The mission of the Circle is and always has been the eradication of the vampire race. Vampires are a cancer on this planet. That hasn't changed. No, the problem I have with the Circle is how they handled the prophecy or whatever you want to call it that I gave them."

"I don't understand." Jim shook his head. "What did they do when you told them there was a vampire left in the world?"

"They sent the wrong guys. I knew the three of them. They were good men, but they were weak."

"How so?"

"They didn't have the strength, the stamina, the…*guts* to take on a vampire." He clenched his fist so tight, his wrinkled knuckles went white. "If you are going face to face with a vampire, you have to be prepared for anything. Those creatures will take the fight to you. They'll tear the flesh from your bones, and you need to be able to take it and keep on fighting. Those men were soft. They never had a chance. There are some in that group who are stronger, but it didn't matter. The ones who went were chosen so that they could have a legacy or glory or something. They wanted to be remembered as heroes. Now they're failures."

Jim scratched his head. "They had the sword."

Simon pushed through another coughing fit, shaking his head and frowning. "That was what they said. Every big flowery statement they made before they left talked about how they had that sword. '*This cut down their ancestors,*' blah blah blah. Stupid. That sword is only powerful if you know how to use it. It doesn't help anyone who is weak. Yes, it counters a vampire's powers, but you have to be strong enough to finish the job. They put too much faith in that sword. They underestimated the girl because they viewed her as the teenager she appeared to be. That's why they're dead."

Here we go. He better have an answer for me. "That vampire you saw, the one they went out to hunt down— what was her name?"

Simon stared into the air above Jim's head for a moment. "I didn't know. I only knew what she looked like and her location. They had to dig around online for her.

They told me it was Victoria Hewitt. That much, I remember. I'll never forget it."

And there it was. Jim needed that information more than anything else in the world. "Why couldn't the Circle have told me that?"

Simon scoffed. "They were afraid of you. They're all scared. Soft. They figured they'd pass the buck to me. They're such cowards, they sent you to a man in his nineties and hoped you'd kill me while they got away. And hey, if you want to, go ahead."

Jim shook his head. "You gave me the information I came for. Why would I kill you?" He paused for a moment and looked deep into Simon's eyes. "That thing you said about the sword—that it doesn't help anyone who is weak."

"Yes?"

"Do you think I'm weak?"

Simon leaned on the armrests of the chair and eyed Jim. "I don't know you. Maybe? You could be. I have no clue."

"I have the sword."

"Okay."

"I found it in a field where I think the Circle encountered this vampire girl. I can finish what they started. I *have* to."

Simon sniffed. "Why?"

"Because my career—my *life*—depends on getting my hands on her. I need to take her out of American society, and I believe I can do that. I've worked my whole life for this, and it's my time to make it a reality. I have nothing left to live for."

Simon rubbed his eye. "They've all worked their lives for it. You're, what, in your thirties? Forties? The Circle has been trying to do it for five hundred years. They get close, but the vampires always seem to win in the end."

"Does that mean you've given up?"

"I'll be dead before any more vampires are killed, son. It doesn't matter to me as much. I've contributed what I can. Maybe we just need new blood in the Circle to continue its legacy. In the meantime, they're just *The Circle* in name only."

Jim stood up. "I appreciate you taking the time to speak with me, Simon. I'm different from those others who failed. I know where Victoria Hewitt is, and I am going to take her down. It's my destiny."

Simon nodded, amused by the dramatics. "Whatever you say. I hope you're right. I'll be rooting for you from here. Just be careful. Vampires have a way of overpowering you when you least expect it. When you have your shot, take it. And good luck, because you're going to need it."

CHAPTER FOUR

Vickie's heart raced as she gingerly walked through the doors of the back entrance of Clear Lake High School. Her arms hung stiffly at her sides. She didn't move her neck. Her eyes were as wide as dinner plates.

Alexis watched her carefully. "Are you sure you're okay?"

"I'm fine. I'll be fine. It's…fine."

Alexis shook her head in disbelief. "You look like you were in a car accident and are wearing a neck brace. At least move your head."

"No sudden movements."

Alexis spoke in a hushed tone. "Is moving your head a sudden movement? You're making it really obvious that something is wrong."

The two girls stopped in front of Vickie's locker. Vickie grabbed the knob to the combination lock and closed her eyes, steadying herself. "I just can't move freely. What's going to give me away more, a stiff neck, or accidentally putting my hand through somebody's ribcage?"

Leaning against the bank of lockers next to her, Alexis clutched the straps of her backpack and leaned her head back. "You've got a point there. Maybe you should have stayed home."

Vickie carefully turned the knob until she heard the *click* of her locker unlocking, then lifted the latch. "And do what? I'd feel the exact same way there, and it's not going to get any better."

Alexis sighed. *This is stupid. She's never going to make it. She looks like her head's going to explode.*

"Why don't you go get ready for the day?" Vickie asked. "You don't want to be late."

"What about you?"

"I'll be fine. Really. Look, here comes Eric. He can keep me going."

"Are you going to tell him how you're feeling?"

"No. I'll come up with something. Just go."

Alexis greeted Eric as their paths crossed, and the boy approached Vickie cautiously. "Hey, babe. How are you feeling?"

Vickie mustered a weak smile. "I'm good. How are you?" She closed the locker and turned to walk with him, again not moving her neck.

"I'm fine." He watched her step slowly through the hall, her eyes fixed forward. "Are you sure you're good? You're walking weird."

She smiled and waved her hand. "Oh. I just, I slept funny last night, and now my neck is all sore and stiff. What are you going to do, you know?"

He lowered his voice. "I didn't know that sort of thing could happen to…you know. Like, can't you just fix that?"

Yes, I can. Shoot. Come up with something. "Well, I can fix injuries. This is more of a strain, which isn't something I can just snap my fingers and make better. I have to wait this one out."

Eric shrugged. *I guess I have a lot to learn about vampires.*

Later that morning, Vickie sat stiff-backed in her Physical Science class. Mr. Bilitz, the teacher, clapped his hands as the last students filtered into the room. "I've got a surprise today, everybody! We're going to play a little game. We've got the big final exam coming up soon, and this is normally the time when we sit around and review old stuff, I let you ask questions, and those of you who know everything already get bored out of your minds. Instead, today, we're going to have a little competition." He turned on the projector, shining a giant crossword puzzle onto the screen in front of the class.

Megan Fitz sneered. "A crossword puzzle? That's your *fun idea?*" A few students scoffed along with her.

"Hey, hear me out." Mr. Bilitz stepped in front of the projector with a smile on his face. "Here's how it's going to work. I'm drawing a line down the middle of the room. Left side will be Team One, and right side will be Team Two. You'll get a point for each correct answer, and there will be opportunities to steal from the other team if they get a wrong answer. Each question on this puzzle will be on the exam. I'll tally up the points at the front of the room, and we'll see who has the most after a few rounds." He looked at the clock. "The last period made it through three rounds before the bell rang, so we've got time."

Another student raised their hand. "What's at stake? Are we competing for anything?"

Mr. Bilitz flashed a dramatic look on his face. "Pride. Respect." Several students booed. "And pizza."

"Pizza?"

"You got it. The winning team will get pizza delivered here by me on exam day. You can take your exam while eating good pie and downing a soda or two. How's that for stakes?"

The room buzzed with anticipation.

"We'll go up and down the rows. Everyone will have opportunities to answer the questions, so it's a true team effort. Anybody caught cheating by whispering answers or trying to look them up will lose a point for their team. Let's go!"

The game was competitive, with both teams scoring early points and stealing a few from the other team. Up and down the rows they went.

Vickie, however, enjoyed none of it. Every time she looked around the room, she felt like someone was watching her. Out of the corner of her eye at one point, she saw a black-shrouded figure. Her head snapped in that direction, only to discover nothing was there at all. *My imagination is going haywire. This is ridiculous.* She shook her head and tried to refocus her energy on the game.

Sweat rolled down the side of her head. Vickie tried to wipe it away without drawing any attention to herself, but she struggled to stay cool. Her hands were still shaking, and her skin was pale. She appeared ready to pass out.

"Okay, now we've come to Vickie." Mr. Bilitz announced, pointing to the projector screen. "Sixteen-down: *A type of water contaminated by human activities.*"

Vickie didn't hear the clue. She was too busy investigating the shadows out of the corner of her eye to notice. Once she realized the room was silent and everyone was staring at her, she looked at the screen. Mr. Bilitz was pointing to sixteen-down, where the first half of the word was blank, but a *W, T,* and *R* were filled in from other crossword answers.

"Oh. Um, freshwater," she answered confidently, but immediately backpedaled when she heard groans coming from her side of the room. "I mean, *polluted water!*"

Mr. Bilitz winced. "Sorry, Vickie, we have to accept your first answer, which would be *freshwater*, and that is incorrect. Team Two, she gave you the answer. Who wants to take it for the steal?"

The rest of Team One, including Megan Fitz, stared at Vickie in disbelief.

"Geez, Vickie, I thought you were *smart!*"

"Where's your head?"

"There goes our pizza!"

Sure enough, Team Two won the competition and the pizza for their final exams. Vickie wouldn't know, because she spent the rest of the contest darting her eyes at anything and everything that moved.

Her clothes clung to her sweat-soaked skin, and her hands trembled violently. *My stomach feels like it's twisted in a knot.* She pushed and pressed on different sides of her stomach, trying in vain to massage some relief into it.

When the bell rang, Vickie snapped out of her daze and back into reality. The rest of the students in Team One got up from their desks, some of them glaring at her with disappointed looks on their faces.

"You okay, Vickie?" Mr. Bilitz turned off the projector

and wheeled it to the side of the room. "You seemed like you weren't on your game today."

"Oh. I'm okay, Mr. Bilitz. Thanks." She stood up from her desk and slung her backpack on her shoulders, hanging her head low as she headed for the door.

"Whatever's on your mind, I hope you can take care of it soon." He wrapped the power cord around the hook on the side of the projector. "If you are this preoccupied during exams, you're not going to be able to think straight. Hang in there."

She didn't look at him. "Thanks."

As she walked out of the room, Vickie was confronted by a waiting Megan Fitz. "Seriously? 'Freshwater?' I may not like you, but you're smarter than that, Vickie."

"Whatever, Megan."

"Did you forget how to read or something? I feel like the word 'contaminated' made it pretty clear."

"Uh-huh."

"Or maybe you just didn't want pizza. That must be it. Watching your figure? It's just about swimsuit season. It makes sense. I appreciate you were thinking of your health, but the rest of us could really go for a good pizza while tackling our exams. Oh, well. Nothing like making half the class hate you." Megan shook her head as she turned right and jogged up the stairs to her next class.

Vickie watched her walk away, and ground her teeth. The fangs poked out, and she quickly covered them with her lips. *Why are these coming out? Just for Megan? Come on, she's just annoying, but she doesn't pose any threat!*

Trying to relax, Vickie walked over to the water fountain, bent over, and twisted the knob on the side. Water shot into the air, then soared even higher. *What the heck?* To Vickie's surprise, the knob was in her hand. She had unwittingly broken it off, and now that water was nearly hitting the ceiling.

Other students began laughing at her, and the stream of water crashed down on the top of her head, soaking her hair and plastering it to her forehead.

One of the teachers ran out into the hall to see what the commotion was and calmly twisted the knob under the fountain to cut off the water.

Vickie stood in front of him, dripping water onto the tile floor, the broken knob in her hand.

The teacher took it from her. "How did this happen?"

"I have no idea. I just went to take a drink like I always do, and it just fell off."

He nodded. "This is an old water fountain anyway. It was probably due to be replaced. I'm not surprised it's starting to fall apart."

Vickie nodded and excused herself to the bathroom to dry her hair. She knew the knob hadn't broken because it was old. It had broken because her powers were flaring up.

In all the distraction, Vickie could feel her fangs extending, but the tightness and pain in her stomach remained. She couldn't do anything about it, and now her hair was wet.

At this point, I should just beg the world to attack me. Let's get this over with so I can move on with my life again.

CHAPTER FIVE

Jim Trembo sat in a cafe, looking out at passersby on the street in Salzburg. He sipped a hot cup of black coffee, trying to warm his insides after walking around in the rain.

He shook his head. *You've been this close before.*

His phone rang, and he pulled it out of his pocket and looked at the screen. It was Pete Stabone.

"Pete! How are you?"

"I'm home, and that's all you need to know about how I'm doing."

Jim laughed. "The wife and kids missed you, eh?"

"Oh, you have no idea. Being back here and getting a little normalcy in my life is a good thing. Nice to not be working out of a suitcase. How are things going out there in Salzburg?"

Jim played with the handle on his coffee cup as he talked. "Well, I'm still living out of a suitcase, so there's that."

"Right. But are you getting anywhere? Have you met up with these guys, or what?"

"Yeah. I've got the name of the girl." He lowered his voice. "I already know she goes to Clear Lake High School since I've found her in the yearbook. It's a shoo-in, man."

"Wasn't a wasted trip, then."

"Far from it." He took another sip of coffee. "But I can't shake the feeling that I'm still on the wrong road."

"What do you mean? Like, you've got the wrong girl?"

"No, just that I…I don't know. It feels weird to be here, I guess."

Pete understood the feeling. "It's just because you're far from home. I was feeling that in Milwaukee for a while, too. Everything is a little different. And shoot, you're in a different country. A completely different part of the world. As long as you are making progress, that's what's important. Just keep doing what you're doing. As you've told me, this one is a sure thing. You're almost at the finish line, so keep going."

Jim sighed. "We've had sure things in the past."

"Not like this, Jim. We have concrete evidence, and have been working off straight facts every step of the way. You're not operating based on what somebody else is telling you. You saw that video with your own eyes."

"Maybe I'm just… I don't trust myself. I can't let this one be it, you know? I can't come all this way and fail. If I do, I have nothing left. I've staked my entire career on this."

"I know you have, Jim. That's why you should be excited that it is coming together so nicely. The United States Government is going to throw you a huge party once you bring her in."

After he hung up, Jim picked up his mug and downed the last of his coffee. Saying that he had staked his entire career on this was not an exaggeration.

After returning the mug to the counter and stepping out into the cold, rainy air once again, Jim's thoughts went back to the last time he'd had a sure thing.

Years earlier, he'd walked through the doors of the Pentagon on an unusually-sunny day for November. He scanned his ID badge several times as he made his way through the stark corridors and deeper into the basement of the building.

His heart had been beating out of his chest that day. A well-meaning coworker sidled up next to him as he power-walked through the Pentagon.

"Big day, Jim?"

"Biggest presentation of my life, Steve. Years of work came down to this."

Steve slapped him on the back. "Go get 'em today. You're going to do great."

Jim scanned his ID a few more times, unlocking various doors until he was finally deep enough in the Pentagon building watching closely as he walked to make sure no one was following him. One final scan opened a door that led to a cold stainless steel laboratory.

Laid out on a long steel table was a man's body, facing the ceiling. Leaning over the body was an older gentleman with long, stringy gray hair and frameless glasses. With a little flashlight, he was peeking into the eyes.

"We got a fresh one?"

The older man startled. "Geez, Jim, you scared me!" He walked over to him, laughing more brightly than most people did while sharing a room with a corpse. "Yeah, this one just went yesterday. He's very intact. I like it. He'll be the perfect prototype for the demonstration."

"I hope you're right. Is this the freshest corpse you've worked with?"

"Oh, goodness, yes. The ones I usually get from, say, the cemetery are already decomposed pretty well, and even embalmed. Makes things trickier. A good, fresh one like this is going to work beautifully."

Jim leaned over the body and looked into the man's face. "Looks like a rather healthy male in his mid-twenties. Average build. How did he die?"

"Self-inflicted gunshot wound."

"We've repaired the damage?"

"Oh, yeah." The older man smiled, and the unsettling glint in his eye made Jim's stomach churn. "We've swapped out everything necessary. All that's left is to turn him on." He stepped over to an IV rack with several bags of fluid hanging off it. Three different tubes extended from the bags to a port attached to the corpse's chest. "And this is our on switch."

Jim straightened, put one hand on his hip, and used the other to scratch his face. "And you're sure this is going to work?"

"Every trial I've done has been successful, Mr. Trembo." He placed his hands on Jim's shoulders. "You've got to relax. This is a sure thing."

Looking back on the memory, Jim shook his head. *I should have known I was screwed. The man was lying to my face without remorse or hesitation.*

He climbed onto the bus and took a seat in the back,

waiting for it to leave the city proper of Salzburg and take him back to the hotel.

He leaned his head against the cold window and thought back to when it had all fallen apart.

"You're smiling an awful lot." Jim shot a worried glance at the old man.

He chuckled. "Well, sir, this is really exciting." His mouth hung open in a seemingly-permanent smile. "This is my opportunity to show the world's most powerful people the work that has been my life for decades. I am just so appreciative you gave me this opportunity."

"Yeah, well, don't screw it up. I wouldn't use the word 'exciting.' We're here in an attempt to play God in front of the President of the United States. If we fail, you get to go back to your farm in the middle of nowhere. *I* will have to deal with the consequences. So please, hold off on the excitement."

"Yes, sir."

Just then, the door flew open and in walked four men clad in dark suits. They were followed by a team surrounding the gentleman in the middle, who sported a red tie and a navy-blue suit. He stepped forward and shook hands with Jim. "Mr. Trembo, it's a pleasure to meet you."

"The pleasure is all mine, Mr. President. Thank you for coming."

The President smiled. "Well, I've heard some interesting things about what you're doing down here. I'm excited to see what you've been able to generate."

"Well, as you know, sir, I am not a scientist. I am the head of the department. But I have been assured that we are getting unbelievable results, and I am thrilled to show you today."

"Sounds good. Let's do it."

The old man stepped forward and shook the President's hand almost violently, trying in vain to contain his excitement and enthusiasm for the moment he was having. "Mr. President, it is a real honor. I have long dreamed of an opportunity to show you my work, and I can't believe the day is today."

"Okay. Settle down, buddy." The President pushed off his hand and gave him a playful shove. "Let's see what you can do."

"Yes, well..." The older man stepped over to the body on the table. "Thank you all for coming. Here we have a deceased man of twenty-three years. He committed suicide by gunshot in the last forty-eight hours, so he is a prime candidate for what I am about to do." He grabbed leather straps and tossed one to Jim. "Mr. Trembo, if you would please help me secure the body to the table."

While complying, Jim looked at the old man. "Why are we doing this?"

"We're bringing somebody back to life, Mr. Trembo. Sometimes these bodies don't take to the idea too well. It's good to have him under control while we wait for the cocktail to take effect."

The President pointed to the IV bags. "Is that the 'cocktail?'"

"Yes, sir!" He pointed to each hanging bag. "This one is a proprietary blend. Well, they *all* are, actually. This one is going to bring the life back into his body. This one here is going to go straight to his brain, sort of defusing him. This is what allows us to control the body. Mr. Trembo has informed me we are doing this for military use. That's what this bag will do. The third bag is just for general healing and wellbeing. A body that's been dead has shut everything down. This brings up a few things the first bag can't on its own."

The President crossed his arms. "Are there any ethical problems? Things we need to be considering?"

Jim shook his head. "To the best of our knowledge, no. According to all the reports that I've been handed, this turns the body into a sort of vehicle. These aren't *people*. They're human robots, essentially."

"So why use this instead of building robots?"

Jim crossed his arms, mirroring his boss. "Well, Mr. President, the thought process is that there are fewer ways for this to go wrong. A robot can be hacked and re-programmed. It can malfunction. Also, you and I both know a fully-functioning human will beat a robot every time."

It didn't take long for the operation to fail.

The old man turned on the IVs, and the fluids ran down their respective tubes until they reached the port. The bags emptied quickly, and so did Jim Trembo's hopes.

As Jim stepped off the bus in front of the hotel, he couldn't shake the feeling of failure that had permeated his entire being as the experiment failed in front of his eyes. He remembered it like it was that day.

The old man had pleaded for another chance. He swore up and down that he had been successful in the past, and just needed time to tweak the process.

Some of the men ushered him out of the room. The

President walked up to Jim, cocked an eyebrow, and shook his head. "We have spent hundreds of thousands of dollars on this. You skipped the protocol. You assured everyone that this was going to work without taking any of the necessary steps to verify it *would* work the way you wanted it to. Tell me why I shouldn't fire you on the spot and shut down your entire department? You have had nothing to show us for years."

"Just give me the weekend, sir. I'll have something for you on Monday, and we can discuss it."

As Jim ascended the elevator to his hotel room, he laughed at the sheer gall he'd had, asking for a second meeting with the President after thoroughly humiliating himself.

He packed his bag in his room, stuffing the last of his dirty laundry inside and zipping it closed. Jim checked his watch and walked over to the window, gazing out at the mountains of Austria.

This project is your savior. It was what kept the department open, and kept your career alive. You can't embarrass yourself again. You're going back to Milwaukee, you're getting that girl, and you're delivering her to the Pentagon. No more playing around. This is your last opportunity to make it.

CHAPTER SIX

Clear Lake High School had a different energy on
exam days.

At the end of each semester, the school operated on a
regular schedule, but the only thing the students did was
take final exams. The buzz in the halls was palpable;
hundreds of students were anxious to get the paperwork
out of the way and be free to go on vacation and get away
from that dreaded building.

Some students didn't care, spending their time
wandering the halls, cracking jokes, and reminiscing about
the past year. Other students couldn't relax, burying their
noses in books, huddled in corners, trying to cram as much
knowledge into their brains as they could before it was
time to be tested.

The different energy made for a fun, interesting time
for the students. It was a novelty in an environment that
was painfully monotonous for long stretches of the school
year.

When Vickie walked in, the energy threw her off even

more than she already was. Jamie saw her walking through the door and approached her with a concerned look on her face.

"Holy cow, Vickie, are you okay?"

Vickie had gotten pretty good at lying about it. "I'm fine. How are you?"

"Fine. But look at you! You're pale and sweaty, and you have bags under your eyes. You look like you haven't slept for three days!"

A week, actually. "Just…nervous about finals, that's all."

"Well, you have nothing to be nervous about. You're a smart girl. I'm sure you're going to do great. Besides, if you go into tests this nervous, you're almost guaranteed to do badly on them. Take a few deep breaths, and maybe splash some cold water on your face to perk yourself up. Are you eating?"

More than anyone can possibly know. "Oh, yeah. Definitely eating. It's okay. I'll be fine."

"Please take care of yourself. You don't want to be laid up in bed to start summer vacation!" She giggled and walked away.

Vickie was taking deep breaths, but they weren't working. The threat she felt was getting closer, and it made her feel increasingly anxious and in pain.

Speaking of eating... Vickie stopped at her locker, pulled it open, and propped up her backpack on her knee. Reaching into the bag, she scooped out two bags of chocolate peanut butter cups, a summer sausage, a box of crackers, a loaf of bread, a package of sandwich meat, and a two-liter bottle of Pepsi.

Vickie had stopped at the supermarket before she got to

school. *The only way I'm getting through this day is by fueling my body as much as possible.* She tossed all the food onto the top shelf of her locker, then stocked up the school supplies in her backpack before zipping it and slinging it over her shoulders again.

Looking both ways in the hall to make sure nobody was watching, Vickie twisted open the loaf of bread and peeled back the packaging on the sandwich meat. *Thank goodness everyone around here has their noses buried in books.* She slipped a few slices of meat between two slices of bread and closed the packages.

The bottle of soda hissed as she twisted off the cap. *A little early to be drinking soda, but you have to do what you have to do.* Vickie chomped down on the sandwich, eating it as fast as she could. Between bites, she lifted the two-liter bottle to her lips and guzzled down some soda, hoping desperately that she could force the hunger pangs to go away.

After she ate the last bite of her sandwich, she took one more deep swig of soda. Just then, Mrs. Braun, one of the English teachers, stopped in front of her with a disgusted look on her face.

"Are you really drinking soda like that?"

Vickie tried to think fast, looking down at the bottle, and then back at the teacher. "I…don't like coffee, and I was up late studying."

Mrs. Braun shook her head. "Exam weeks…"

Vickie did her best to ignore her panicked state during the first few exams of the day. The food helped, but not much. She was sweaty and exhausted, doing anything she could to keep from showing signs of distress.

By the time she reached Physical Science class, it had spilled out of control once again.

Not that the atmosphere helped.

When she walked into the classroom, somebody had printed out a picture of a dirty pond with garbage floating in it and a tire sticking out of it and written *FRESHWATER* in capital letters above it. They'd taped it to the whiteboard so that everyone saw it as they walked in.

There were snickers as she walked up to it. On the one hand, she was so distracted, she almost couldn't react to it. But then again, it gave her a chance to lash out, even if it was just at a piece of paper.

Without looking at her laughing classmates, Vickie ripped the paper off the board and crumpled it into a ball. Despite the wastebasket being on the other side of the classroom, she reared back and launched the wad. The paper ball rocketed like a bullet across the room, striking the wall behind the wastebasket so hard that it partially flattened on impact.

The snickering stopped. Vickie took her seat, closed her eyes, and tapped her foot while she waited for the exam to start.

Before the Physical Science exam, she'd stopped at her locker and taken several large bites out of the summer sausage, interspersed with crackers. To onlookers, it was disgusting, but during Exam Week, everyone understood that each student was doing what they needed to do to survive.

Her hunger was reasonably under control...until the pizza arrived.

Mr. Bilitz waltzed into the room with a satisfied smile

on his face and three boxes of hot takeout pizza in his arms. Plates and napkins were piled on top of the boxes. On the far countertop of the classroom, several bottles of soda were waiting next to a stack of plastic cups.

The students who were part of the winning crossword puzzle team eagerly leaped from their seats to fill plates and pour cups. One by one, they returned to their desks with steam rising into the air from the melted cheese on each plate.

And just like that, Vickie was hungry again.

Her mouth watered, adding another distraction as she began taking her exam. Her handwriting was shaky and crooked. She continued to take deep breaths, to the point where other students were getting distracted by them.

The words on the page started to melt together. Some of them danced, and others flipped around. What had been a standard science test turned into a garbled mess, indecipherable to her eyes.

Vickie sat up straight and looked at the rest of the class. Everyone else had their heads down, dutifully finishing their exams. She still wasn't past the second question.

She lowered her head and tried to refocus. She repeatedly blinked in a vain attempt to straighten out the jumble of words, numbers, and shapes.

A bead of sweat rolled down the center of her forehead, between her eyes, and down to the tip of her nose, where it rested for a moment before silently splattering on the page.

Vickie sighed loudly, and several classmates flashed her confused and frustrated looks.

She began to make sense of the second question. It had something to do with calculating the density of an object.

Okay, you know this one. Density equals mass divided by volume.

But once she brought the tip of her pencil down to the page and dragged it across, the tip exploded, tearing the paper and making her pencil useless.

Vickie pushed herself up, feeling the room spinning around her. Clumsily, she got up from her desk and stumbled to the front of the room.

Mr. Bilitz was surprised when he looked up and saw her. "Vickie," he whispered, "you look terrible. Are you feeling okay?" She still had sweat lines on her forehead, and seemed disoriented and struggling to keep it together.

"No." She shook her head, trying to choke back her tears of frustration. "May I be excused to the bathroom?"

The teacher leaned over to look down the row of desks. Vickie's backpack was still on the floor by her desk.

"Okay. Take care of yourself."

"Thank you." With another deep breath, Vickie walked out the door and into the empty, cavernous hallway. A chill ran up her spine, reminding her that the Science Wing of the school was better air-conditioned than everywhere else. Her sweat nearly froze, and she shivered as she jogged down the hall to the bathroom.

Every step there felt awkward and wobbly, as though she were running across the deck of a ship being tossed on the waves of the ocean. Thankfully, nobody was around to see it.

Once inside the bathroom, Vickie made sure the coast was clear. There were three stalls, and none of them were occupied. She flipped the deadbolt to lock out anybody who might try to come in.

Her feet dragged as she approached the mirror and leaned on the sink counter to steady herself. *Look at you! Your eyes are bloodshot, and your hair is a mess. Your makeup is a disaster. There is no color in your skin. Why can't you get hold of yourself?*

The pain in her stomach twisted tighter, to the point where she fell to the cold tile floor of the bathroom, clutching her midsection and groaning quietly. Tears streamed from her eyes. *Whatever is coming, why can't it just get here already? Enough of this!*

While lying on the floor, she slipped her phone out of her pocket. Remembering that Alexis had a free period this hour, she unlocked her phone and fired off a text.

I need you. Please

She hated being so melodramatic. But Vickie also didn't know what else to do. Her phone buzzed in response, and the two had a quick conversation:

What's going on?

I can't keep it together. Losing control

Oh man

Where are you?

The girls' bathroom in the Science Hall

Okay, I'm on my way. Just stay low

Vickie smirked at the instruction, figuring she couldn't get much lower than lying on the bathroom floor.

Soon, there was a knock at the door. "Vickie, it's me. Let me in."

Vickie rolled onto her stomach and pushed herself onto all fours. Once there, she pulled herself up using the counter. The room continued spinning, but she was able to stumble over to the door and unlock it for her friend.

Alexis pushed her way in and took one look at Vickie. "Good grief, you look like death. Is this still the same thing as before?"

Vickie closed her eyes, trying to focus on what her instincts were attempting to tell her. Unfortunately, it didn't work. "I don't know. I just can tell it's bad. I'm never going to make it through exams like this."

Alexis walked Vickie across the bathroom and sat her down on a short bench by the door. She leaned her head against the wall to keep her body from spiraling completely out of control.

"Have you broken anything yet?"

"No." Vickie closed her eyes and let the cool of the tile wall calm her. "I was barely able to make it here, though. I'm worried I'm going to break something. I can't last much longer."

Alexis placed her hand on Vickie's shoulder. "Okay. Let's get you a snack and a drink of water. Maybe that will help. Stay in here. I've got a granola bar in my locker."

As she watched Alexis slip out of the bathroom, Vickie clamped her eyes shut. *Mutter. Vater. What can I do? Am I cursed to be like this for the rest of my life?*

CHAPTER SEVEN

For the rest of the period, Vickie and Alexis sat on the bench in the girls' bathroom as Vickie choked down the granola bar and guzzled water.

"I don't know what else to do." Vickie shook her head, looking down at the last bite of her granola bar. "I can't survive this."

Alexis gave her a puzzled look. "Seriously?"

"Look at me, Alexis! I'm a mess. I can't take my exams. I'm going to fail a class because my instincts are all over the place, and that's even if I make it that long. This is no way to live."

Alexis leaned back and crossed her legs. "Let me get this straight. The girl sitting in front of me who survived being attacked by people who tried to cut off her head? The girl who survived in a coffin buried underground for centuries? *That girl* is ready to throw in the towel because she's worried she's going to fail an exam? Give me a break!"

"It's not just the exam." Vickie crumpled the empty wrapper. "How can I do anything? Even if this were back in my era, this tightness and pain in my stomach is keeping me from functioning. I wouldn't be able to milk a goat with this pain, or deliver anything to town. I'd be stuck in my room, not allowed to leave under any circumstances. There's never been anything like this. This pain, this…I don't know. It is driving me crazy."

"You want to know what's going on out there right now?" Alexis pointed to the door. "There are hundreds of students. All of them are going through the same thing you are."

Vickie cocked an eyebrow. "Oh, are all of those kids also worried about being beheaded or attacked by a vicious group of cultists? Do they all need to be concerned about whether they're going to live through the night?"

"Okay, I get your point, but let me pull back a little bit. Every student in this school is trying to do the same thing you are: survive. They are trying to get decent grades on their exams. They're dealing with drama at home. Some of them have awful relationships they're trying to figure out. No, they're not dealing with literal life-or-death situations, but in high school, *everything* is life-or-death. They're figuring out ways to take their exams while they're sick, or while distracted by their parents' divorce, or whatever. If they can figure it out, so can you."

"What about my Physical Science exam? I'm supposed to take it right now. The period is almost over."

Alexis spoke calmly. "You're going to go to Mr. Bilitz and tell him you got sick and threw up. They can't do anything about that, and it's an airtight excuse. He'll set up a time with you during one of your free periods to come back and take the exam. Bilitz is one of the cooler teachers here. You'll be okay."

Vickie wiped the sweat from her brow and took a sip of water. "Thanks for bringing this stuff and talking to me. I'm sorry if I interrupted anything."

Alexis giggled. "I was in the practice room in the Choir Hall trying to learn how to play the *Pink Panther* theme on the piano. You didn't interrupt anything."

"Good." The bell rang. "I guess I need to get to my locker and switch out my books."

Vickie thanked Alexis one more time and unlocked the bathroom door before heading back out into the sea of people. Remembering her backpack was still in the classroom, Vickie walked back. Her eyes drooped in a combination of sadness and exhaustion as she quietly picked it up.

Mr. Bilitz emerged from a back closet. "Vickie! Are you doing okay?"

"Uh, yeah. I'm doing fine. Is there a way I can make up this test?"

He put his hands on his hips. "I don't believe in punishing a student just because he or she gets sick, even on an exam day. Let me know your open hours, and you can come back here and take the test."

Once the two of them worked out the makeup test, Vickie hurried out to get to her locker. *I have to switch out to my US History books before the next period.*

She jogged across the skywalk connecting the Science Hall with the History Hall, then walked down the stairs to the English Hall where her locker was waiting for her.

But that's not all that was waiting for her.

As Vickie pulled open her locker, she heard a judgmental-sounding sigh from behind her. She dropped her backpack and turned around to see Megan Fitz, of all people, standing with a smirk on her face.

"Boy, Vickie, you didn't look too hot in there. Almost sick. I wasn't sure if you were going to throw up or if you needed something to eat. Too bad you couldn't have any pizza, hey?"

"Megan, now isn't the time." Vickie turned her back to the girl, tossing her science textbook into her locker.

"Do you ever get tired of embarrassing yourself? Like, especially in *that* class. It's like you can't keep yourself together for more than an hour without drawing attention to yourself. Then again, I know how much you like attention."

Vickie shook her head. "I think you're thinking of yourself, Megan. I don't need attention." She rummaged through her locker to find her history book. "Besides, I think the whole reason you don't like me is that I attract attention."

Megan crossed her arms. "Why would that bother me?"

"Because you're used to being the center of attention." Vickie shoved the book into her backpack and zipped it up. "Everyone focuses on you, but then a new girl comes in and takes the attention away from you. Catches people's eyes. That must be hard to take."

Megan lowered her eyes. "Get over yourself."

Vickie spun around. "Me? I've got nothing to get over! I've spent this entire year minding my own business. If it's not you, it's one of your friends. You girls seem totally bent on making me miserable just for existing. I haven't done anything to you, or at least, not without you starting it. Why don't you just back off and leave me alone?"

"You make it so easy sometimes, Vickie." Megan sneered. "At first, we were just hazing you a little. You're the new girl, and that's how it goes. But you reacted with violence against me. For shame." She shook her head disapprovingly. "Shows a real lack of maturity."

Vickie slammed her locker door. "I am getting sick and tired of listening to you judge me and give me a hard time just for being here. I'm not going anywhere, and neither are you, so we better find a way to coexist for the next couple of years."

Megan pursed her lips. "I don't have to coexist with anyone. You don't get to tell me what to do. If you would just respond to things like a normal human being instead of some weird freak who can't keep herself under control, maybe you wouldn't have gotten that answer wrong. And you wouldn't have had to run out of class just now. Are you sick, or are you just freaking out because you were having a hard time with the test?" She stepped forward. "The way I see it, wherever you came from, you were able to just coast by, doing whatever you wanted. Now you're in a new school where things are tougher. You get flustered and you can't handle it, so you lash out. It's immature, and if you want to survive high school, you better start growing up."

Vickie's stomach was still twisted in knots. She did everything she could to keep her fangs from poking out of her mouth. She clamped her lips together, her eyes wide. The way Megan was talking to her, Vickie just wanted to put her fist through her face.

Of course, she couldn't. She was stronger than Megan, and Megan had no idea.

The girl glanced down and saw Vickie ball up her fists. "Oooh, here we go. Are you going to hit me? Go ahead! Do it! You'll get kicked out of school so fast your head will spin. Face it, I'm untouchable. Take your best shot. With all these witnesses around, you don't stand a chance."

Keep it together. Please. Keep it together. Don't let your powers get the better of you. Despite her internal conflict, Vickie couldn't control her rage much longer.

Instead of punching Megan with the full force of her powers and likely committing murder in the middle of the hall in Clear Lake High School, Vickie turned around and unleashed a vicious punch to her locker door.

The impact was epic. The door came off its hinges, almost folding in half. A perfect outline of her fist appeared in the middle of the carnage. With a loud crash, the door fell to the tile floor.

She glared at Megan. Megan stepped forward and surveyed the damage, then looked at Vickie in shock.

Vickie stared her down. "Well? Do you want me to punch you?"

Without saying a word, Megan glanced at the other kids who had congregated around the two of them. They all wore looks of confusion, a few covering their mouths in disbelief.

Megan shoved them out of the way and ran off, leaving Vickie behind as everyone watched her. *Man, that felt good. Even that little bit out of my system makes all the difference in the world.*

She placed her foot on the now L-shaped locker door,

shoving it out of the middle of the hallway and up against the bank of lockers. As she started walking to the stairs, the other students parted, not wanting anything to do with her.

Vickie reached her history class just in time. When she sat down to take her exam, she felt slightly better. Her body was still anxious, but that little bit of release she'd enjoyed from punching the locker had refocused her.

Something was still out there, but at least she could gather her thoughts well enough to take the exam.

Downstairs, several teachers stood around the destroyed locker door after the halls emptied.

"I don't know what to do with this."

"Is that the shape of a fist?"

"I bet one of the football players did this."

"How? I've never seen anything like this before."

"Let's get it out of the way so that nobody gets hurt. We'll find out who did this and hold them accountable."

Two of them picked up the locker door and marched down the hall with it as one of the teachers noted whose locker it was.

Vickie would be charged several hundred dollars to replace the door. After explaining the situation to Craig when he got the call the next day, he told her that he was just glad she didn't hit Megan.

Still, everyone was glad to know that school was just about over so they could get a break from these situations, at least for the time being.

It had been a long school year.

CHAPTER EIGHT

Jim Trembo walked along the sidewalk in front of Clear Lake High School with a spring in his step so strong, he was practically skipping.

You've got everything you need, Jim. Now to just get Victoria Hewitt's address and you're in. This whole thing is in the bag. You did it!

Even though it was Friday, Jim was thrown off by how quiet the building seemed as he approached it.

Doesn't look like anybody is in the classrooms. The few that have lights on are empty. Did I miss the school year? Is it over already?

He buzzed the intercom at the main entrance and heard the door lock unlatch. He walked in and breezed past the front desk, which was not occupied.

As he peered down one of the empty halls, the echoes of his footsteps were unsettling. *Seriously, is anyone even here? Who let me in?*

Jim walked down the hall to Mr. Goede's office and knocked on the door, which was partially open. As it swung open, he saw the principal sitting behind his desk, smiling at him.

"Mr. Trembo, a pleasure to see you, sir." He stood up and extended his hand to shake. "I did not think you were going to be coming back. You just disappeared one day. I figured the US government had called you back for some other important mission."

Jim shook his hand and then looked over his shoulder. "No, I just had more research to do. Who let me in? It doesn't seem like there is anyone here."

The little bald man laughed. "I have a connection to the front door in here. I let you in once I saw you on the camera. There are a handful of faculty members here finishing up some work, but other than that, it's a ghost town here today."

"Did I miss the end of school?" Jim sat down in one of the office chairs on the other side of the desk from Mr. Goede.

The principal shook his head. "It's exam week. We offer a shorter week for our students to help them deal with the excess stress of taking exams. They're off today, but they'll be back for three more days next week. Then, it's summertime."

"Just like that."

"Just like that, Mr. Trembo. That's how school years go, and that's why I'm surprised to see you here. I thought you knew we were going to be off today."

Jim hadn't thought of that. He hadn't even checked into a hotel yet. The second he'd gotten off the plane from Salzburg, he'd rented a car, thrown his things in the back, and driven straight to the school. "I've been in a rush. Didn't look at the calendar."

Mr. Goede slapped his palms on his desk. "Well, I don't know what you'd like to do. I'm here to help, as always. But if you wanted to patrol the hallways and observe students some more, I'm afraid it'll be a few days."

Jim waved his hand. "No, actually. If you can help me, I will have all the information I need."

"That's good." The principal folded his hands. "What is left? What can I help you with?"

"I believe I know who the perpetrator is." Jim leaned in. "I've been able to access intel that pointed me in the right direction. Now I just need the contact information for that student."

Mr. Goede's face showed a mix of excitement and disappointment. "I was hoping I didn't have any students who were involved in performance-enhancing drugs." He sighed. "But that's the world we live in. Who is the student?"

"Well, now, here's the thing. I can't just give you the name of the student. If I do that, I'm inviting some variables into the mix that I can't control. We don't want the word to get around about who we are investigating."

This was a deliberate move on the part of Jim Trembo. The last thing he wanted was to let anyone know who he was investigating. It would likely cause other people to sniff around and impede his progress.

At this point, there was no way he would let anyone else get in his way.

"I'm going to give you a list of students, Mr. Goede. Five

of them, actually, and it is with the understanding that you are not to conduct an investigation of your own. If I give you these names, you are giving me your word that these students are going to be free of any scrutiny on your part."

Mr. Goede stared at him for a moment, mulling over what he was saying. "On the one hand, I understand what you mean, and I respect your desire for privacy. But I am the principal here, and I'd like to know what's going on at my school."

"I'm not in the business of keeping secrets from people who need to know things. Right now, you don't need to know. At least, not until we can investigate this person thoroughly and make our determination first."

The principal sighed. "What are the names?"

Jim thought this out beforehand. A mix of boys' names and girls' names would sufficiently keep the school administration off the scent, he figured. "Alex Consuelos, Steve Schnitker, Eddie Hart, Christina Gilles, Victoria Hewitt, and Kaitlyn Wells."

Mr. Goede frowned as he jotted down the names of the students. "All athletes. Good students, too. This is really disappointing."

"I'd like to urge you to not treat any of these students differently until we have more information, sir. Remember, of the six names I just gave you, five are completely innocent. Their names are just on this list incidentally. Please be sure you treat all the students fairly. I would really hate it if an innocent student was treated like they were guilty on my account."

After tapping at his computer keyboard for a few minutes, Mr. Goede stood up from his desk and walked over to the printer on top of the filing cabinet across the room. He pulled a sheet of paper out of the tray and handed it to Trembo. "Here you go. I hope you find what you're looking for."

Jim smiled as he scanned the sheet until his eyes rested on Victoria Hewitt's information. It was all he could do to not sprint out of the office and go straight to her house. Instead, to keep up appearances, he calmly stood up and shook Mr. Goede's hand. "I'll report back when I have more to tell you. Hang tight."

"Is there a number I can reach you at, Mr. Trembo? I'd like to follow up on this if I don't hear anything."

"Of course." Jim reached into his pocket and produced a small white card. "You can call this number anytime."

Mr. Goede thanked him and returned to his desk while Jim strolled out of the office and down the hall, laughing quietly. *Not that anyone will answer that fake phone number. I love giving that thing out. Farewell, Clear Lake High School.*

Jim Trembo strode to his rental car, eager to pull out his phone and enter the address of the vampire girl. Seeing that she lived north of the school, he could swing through the hotel and check back in on his way, giving him a chance to dump his stuff.

After he claimed his new room, he dragged his bags in and plopped them on the second bed. He unzipped the large duffel bag to reveal the sword that would deactivate Vickie's powers.

I just have to get my hands on her, and this baby will do the rest. Maybe I can bring her here. No, that's no good. I'll need a Plan B. Bringing her here would arouse too much suspicion. He left the sword on the bed. *No sense in bringing that now. I don't want to lug that thing around until I need it. She's just a teenager. I'll grab her and tie her up or something, then I can make my move.*

After stopping at several hardware stores along the way to pick up supplies without being too noticeable, Jim Trembo made his way to the north side of Milwaukee, turning down Green Tree Road with a smile on his face. *This is it, boy. You are on your way.*

He drove past the Watson household. *Okay, third house from the end. Looks like a cemetery across the street. How appropriate for a vampire. I bet she sleeps in there at night or something. Small family ranch home. Maybe I'll set up shop somewhere in the cemetery.*

The plan was to spend time observing the house: when people were going in and out, how often Vickie came and went. He'd formulate a game plan based on that information.

Jim drove around the block until he found the entrance to the Golden Valhalla Cemetery. Slowly, he wove his car down the winding paths of the cemetery before reaching a spot to park. He grabbed a small backpack off the passenger seat and continued on foot.

Nobody's around, so it's a good time to set up. Not wanting to stand for too long, Jim bemoaned the lack of benches in the cemetery. He dropped the backpack next to a headstone marked *FILSON*. He sat down on the headstone, finding that it offered just enough comfort to allow him to stay in one spot for long stretches of time.

With his binoculars in one hand and a sandwich in the other, Jim sat on the headstone, spilling crumbs all over the ground. As he chewed on his last bite, he saw activity in the house. He lifted the binoculars to his eyes.

I see dark hair. That might be our girl. She's wearing some kind of tan shirt with long khaki capris. The guy must be the father of the house. They're getting into a car and driving off. Darn, I wouldn't be able to get back to my car in time to tail them. Oh, well. What time is it? 4:45pm. She might be heading to work.

The sound of a throat clearing snapped Jim out of his concentration. He looked up to see an elderly woman with a look of shock on her face, while her son scowled at him. She was holding flowers.

It didn't take long for Jim to realize what he had done. He leaped to his feet from the headstone and brushed the crumbs off his lap. "I'm so sorry. Um, my condolences to you and your family in this difficult time." They shook their heads as he scurried off to his car. *Maybe I'd better do this at night.*

Later that evening, under the cloak of darkness, Jim Trembo returned to the cemetery. He walked to the *FILSON* headstone, which now hosted the bouquet of flowers the family had placed there earlier in the day.

"Sorry, Filson. I need to do this. I hope you understand."

Jim pulled out a different set of binoculars and flipped a switch on them to activate the night vision mode. Two hours later, he perked up, seeing the SUV return to the driveway. As Vickie and Craig walked to the side door, Jim was able to zoom in on the girl. *She's wearing a shirt for a restaurant. Al's Seafood. Interesting. Maybe she waits tables or something. I'll have to look that up when I get back to the hotel room.*

Nothing else of note happened that evening as Jim Trembo sat perched on the edge of the *FILSON* tombstone. Still, he now had eyes on the girl, knew where she lived, and assumed he knew where she worked.

Just get it to the finish line, Jim. That's all you have to do. The hard part is over.

CHAPTER NINE

"I just want to take a minute to thank all of you who supported *The Truth About...* this season. I've been stunned by how many of you jumped in, shared your stories on our Facebook Page, and listened to my family and me talk about our struggles blending together. Personally, I've had a lot of fun, and it's been very fulfilling for me. Stay tuned to the Facebook Page this summer as we continue to share stories and photos, as well as talk about what's on tap for our next season, which we will release in the fall. Until then, I'm Craig Watson, and always keep an eye out for the truth. We'll see you next time."

Craig switched off his microphone, stopped the recording, and leaned back in his chair. He folded his hands and placed them behind his head, staring at the ceiling. Then he closed his eyes and took a deep breath.

And just like that, the season is over. What a whirlwind.

Indeed, it had been quite a season for Craig and his family. The skyrocketing success of his podcast had produced a viable income stream, comfortably paying the bills from his sponsors' ad fees.

As the audio file uploaded to his cloud storage for safe-keeping, Craig opened his budgeting app and double-checked all the numbers. *With this next episode's fees, we'll be able to top off the Living Expenses fund and keep afloat for three solid months while we record new material and game out the new season. Outstanding!*

He stood up from his desk chair and looked in the mirror. Dark-brown and gray stubble poked out of his cheeks. His hair was messy. Craig pulled his glasses off his face and buffed the smudges off them with the bottom of his old gray sweatshirt. *Geez, Craig, I know it's Saturday, but do you have to look like such a schlub? Then again, where do I have to go?*

Craig double-checked the upload of his audio file. *Don't want to leave until I know it's safely in the cloud.* He paced around his bedroom for a moment, thinking about what he wanted to do that day. *I have to make sure Vickie is okay. It'd be nice to do something fun this afternoon, but Vickie isn't going anywhere, the way she's been feeling. I want to celebrate getting the season done. Maybe some pizza tonight...*

The notification bubble popped up on his computer screen. The upload was done.

Craig nodded, then walked out of his bedroom and headed to the kitchen, where Alexis was standing next to the open dishwasher, stacking plates on the countertop.

"Did you get it done, Dad?"

"Season Three is on the books!" Craig wore a satisfied smile as he stuck his hands into the pockets of his sweatpants.

"Awesome! That's gotta feel good."

"Yeah, it does." He shuffled over to the sliding glass door and stared out into the field behind the house.

"You, uh…you going to *shower* at some point today, Pop?"

Craig looked down at his comfortable-but-drab outfit. "This isn't a good look for me?"

Alexis shrugged as she picked up the stack of plates to put them in the cabinet. "I mean, if you're not planning on being seen by other humans, it's fine."

Such a spitfire. "Nah, I'll shower in a little while. Where's Vickie?"

"She's lying down." His daughter pulled open the top rack of the dishwasher. Water dripped from a cup that flipped over during the wash cycle, splashing her legs. "Ugh, stupid cups. These things never stay straight."

"Vickie's lying down? It's only ten in the morning. She's still not feeling good, hey?"

"Dad, I'm not sure when she's ever going to feel good again." She carefully lifted the water-filled cup and dumped the dishwater into the sink. "I'm afraid it's going to be like this until whatever it is she's dreading hits. She says she started feeling really lousy again last night."

Craig nodded. "When I brought her home after work, I thought I was going to have to carry her into the house. She told me it got worse as we got closer to home. I don't know what to do anymore."

Alexis wiped the cup dry with the towel on her shoulder and put it away in the cupboard. "She says all we can do is keep going about our lives. I'm doing my best. What are your plans for today?"

Craig's voice grew a little louder with a bit of energy and optimism. "I was really hoping we could go out this evening and celebrate. With the new season done, I can pull back on recording for a few months. We can probably sneak in a vacation sometime this summer. I mean, I'll still have work to do while I set up for the next season, but it would be nice to, you know, go do something."

"You totally should!" Alexis raised her eyebrows. "You've worked hard this year. After all we've been through, it's a minor miracle you've been able to keep up with the podcast."

"Well, I don't think any celebrating is happening tonight."

"Why not?"

"We can't go anywhere if Vickie is feeling like this. I'd want to stick around here, just in case she starts to feel worse or anything goes down. It's hard to party when your kids are sick."

Alexis pushed the racks of the dishwasher back into the unit and kicked the door up with the side of her foot. She caught it with her hand, closing it and hanging the dish towel across the handle on the front. "I can always chill here with her and let you know if anything's up. You really do need to go celebrate. You deserve it."

Craig shook his head. "I want to celebrate with somebody. Preferably you girls, since you two are just as much a part of it as I am."

"Oh. I see what you mean. Yeah, I think Vickie would probably bring the party down, then."

He stared out the window, feeling sorry for himself.

"What about that Katie woman?"

Craig looked at his daughter. "Huh?"

"Katie. The girl you ran into at the hardware store. Why not call her and ask her out? The two of you can celebrate. Then you're getting a date out of it, too. Two birds with one stone, right?"

"Sweetheart, I'm not worried about dating right now while there is so much going on here. I was thinking we just order a pizza tonight and stick at home."

Alexis twisted her face in disgust. "Dad, that's lame. She gave you her number. Call her and go get a drink or something. Or at least get a pizza that's not delivery. Us girls can stick around here. You liked her, right?"

Craig stared at his daughter for a moment, trying to gauge the enthusiasm in her eyes. "Yeah. Katie was the one who got away."

"What's that?"

"It's just an expression. When you like someone, and they like you, and you don't get together for some reason, like bad timing, you call them 'the one who got away.' That's Katie to me."

"Okay, well, she's not 'away' anymore, Dad. She's right here, and she's asking you to call her. I say you pick up the phone, give her a call, and see what she's doing tonight."

Vickie shuffled into the kitchen, scraping her heels on the linoleum floor while she held her stomach with both hands. She mustered up a fake smile. "Hey, guys, what are we talking about?"

"Hey, sweetie. How are you feeling?" Craig walked over and put his hand on her shoulder.

"Eh." Vickie shook her head. "It's still there. I'm getting tired of lying around. I want to be doing things."

"Well, I want you to rest." Craig tilted his head in concern. "We still don't know what's causing this, and I'd rather you destroy things around this house instead of going out where you can really do damage if things spiral out of control."

"We were just talking about Dad going out on a date tonight."

"Alexis!"

Vickie looked hopefully at Craig. "Really? With who?"

Craig opened his mouth to reply, but his daughter beat him to it. "An old high school flame. 'The one that got away.'" She waved her arms dramatically as she said it. "This is his chance to see if this girl still likes him."

"Alexis, knock it off."

"I saw the way she looked at you, Dad. She's into you. Call her and go have some fun."

Vickie nodded. "Totally."

"Now hang on a second, girls. That's not how this works, okay? First of all, there's no guarantee Katie wants to go out on a date with me. For all I know, she just wants to be friends, and just gave me her number to be polite. That's it. Let's not put the cart before the horse here." Vickie gave him a confused look, closing one eye. "It's an expression. I just mean, don't move too fast. Second, I'm not going anywhere as long as Vickie is feeling this way."

Vickie opened both eyes wide. "That's not going to fly. If you have things you want to do, go do them. I'm not going to keep you from having a good time. Please don't adjust your life for me."

Craig put his hands on his hips. "You're not feeling well.

I'm your parent. A good parent sticks around when his kids aren't feeling well."

"Yeah, but it's not like I have a cold. This is something different, and my instincts spike all the time for different reasons. I know this seems bad, but you're going to spend the rest of your life adjusting your plans for me if you try to work around every time my instincts are acting up."

Alexis nodded as she rinsed a rag and squeezed the excess water out of it. "She's right. Go call Katie."

"Girls, enough. I'm not calling Katie, okay?"

His daughter tossed the rag onto the countertop, leaned against it, and crossed her arms. "What's really going on here? You're not just avoiding this because of Vickie. I can tell."

Craig avoided eye contact with her. "You can't tell anything."

"Shoot! I'm your daughter. Give me a break."

Vickie pulled over a kitchen chair. "Yeah, what's really the deal? Why won't you call her?"

Craig sighed for a moment. "I don't want to get rejected, okay?"

The girls exchanged empathetic looks. "Seriously?" Alexis grabbed the rag and wiped the crumbs off the counter. "Dad…"

He waved his arms. "Yeah, yeah, that's high school stuff. I get it, but I wasn't prepared for how hard dating would be. It frustrates me like crazy. I'm tired of dealing with all the drama. I feel like a kid, and not in a good way." He pointed to Alexis. "I know all the stuff I told you about people being interested in you and wanting to spend time with you, so just save it. I don't want to hear it right now.

There's too much going on that is frustrating me. I can't go through this over and over. End of discussion."

Vickie shook her head. "You better not be avoiding this because of me."

"I'm not. I'm avoiding it because of *me.* Now, I want to celebrate tonight. We're going to have pizza and hang out. Maybe watch a movie or something. Let's take it easy and stuff our faces with junk food because it's fun, and we've earned it. I think we all just need to chill for a night. Now, if you'll excuse me, I am going to go take a shower."

He walked out of the kitchen.

Alexis draped the rag on the edge of the sink to dry. "He needs to get out."

"I know." Vickie propped her elbow on the table and rested her cheek on her fist. "And so do I."

CHAPTER TEN

Jim Trembo sported a half-smile on his face as he stared at the house in front of him.

Front gutter missing on the right side. One, two...three boarded-up windows I can see. Half the paint is gone. Cracked sidewalk. Broken railing. More bare spots on the roof than shingles. I bet a good, stiff wind would knock this house down in one swoop. It's perfect!

He went up the walkway, dodging the cracks and stubbing his toe on the uneven concrete. The rotted wooden steps creaked under his feet as he strode to the front porch.

Jim spun and placed his hands on the guardrail on the porch, leaning forward to look down the street to check out the "neighbors." A loud creak accompanied the free movement of the railing, and he quickly stood up straight, laughing. *Note to self: don't lean on anything.*

On all sides of him, Jim saw houses in similar states of disrepair. One front lawn was littered with old, decrepit toys. Another held a pile of broken beer bottles. Across the street, a bright orange sticker on the front door told onlookers that the house was condemned.

A honking horn caught Jim's attention, and he waved at the white sedan that pulled up in front of the house. Out stepped a young man in a light-blue button-down shirt and khaki pants, swiping on his phone as he pushed the driver's side door shut.

Jim estimated the boy couldn't have been more than two or three years out of college. *He has the confidence of a child. Optimistic, but cautious. He doesn't sell too many houses in this area.*

"Mr. Trembo?"

"Call me Jim." He extended his hand. "You must be Brad."

"Yes, sir. Nice to meet you, Jim. Let me just go ahead and unlock the door here." The boy stepped to the front door and punched in the combination on the lock strapped to the doorknob.

"Yeah, we don't want anyone breaking into this one and trying to steal stuff, am I right?" Jim snickered.

"Well, I doubt you have much of that going on in this neighborhood. Unfortunately, you get a lot of squatters around here." Brad pulled apart the lock and pushed the flimsy wooden door open. "A good rainy night and anyone out on the street is going to be looking for shelter. That, and kids like to come in and trash the place."

Jim smiled when he walked in and saw the state of affairs inside the house. "Looks like they already got to this one!"

What had once been a nice hardwood floor had deteriorated into gaping holes and piles of sawdust. Wallpaper curled and hung off the walls in spots. The plaster on the walls was cracked and disintegrated as they walked into the house.

Brad didn't seem too optimistic. "I'd give you a rundown of the place, but you already saw the photos. Do you have any questions for me?"

Jim did his best to look like he was interested in the details. "So this is a three-bedroom, two-bath?"

Brad nodded. "Yep. Although it's plumbed for two bathrooms, both will need to be ripped out completely."

"I imagine most things would be at this point."

Jim moved ahead and stepped into the kitchen. All the appliances were missing. "I guess either the previous homeowners took their appliances with them or this place was ransacked."

"Either/or. You're not going to find appliances included in a place around here."

Looking up at the holes in the ceiling, Jim tilted his head quizzically. "Doesn't look like there's anything up there. Why would they cut into the ceiling like that?"

"There's not anything up there *anymore*. Around here, some of the craftier—let's call them *visitors*—dig into the walls and ceilings and pull out any copper pipe they find. They can take that down and cash it in. Older homes like these are loaded with it, so it's a safe bet that's what happened here."

"So, I should get a good security system, then?" Jim winked.

Brad chuckled. "At the very least." He leaned back and glanced down the short hall off the kitchen. "If you don't mind me asking, what drew you to this house in particular?"

Jim kicked a pile of debris in the middle of the kitchen with the side of his foot. "The price tag, to be honest. You're not going to find too many houses in today's market at this low price."

"You're right about that, Jim, but you get what you pay for with these houses."

"I want a fixer-upper."

"This might be a little more *fixer* than *upper* for you."

"You'd be surprised." *Look natural. Ask some more typical questions.* "What are the comps in the neighborhood like?"

Brad pulled up the listing on his phone. "Let's take a look. I see a couple on this street that sold for about $40,000. That's not too bad, but that was also the peak, and it was in a seller's market. You're going to spend $40,000 on this place just to clean it up and get it ready for fixing up."

Jim waved his hand. "I'm not worried about that. Is this the bathroom over here?" He stuck his head in and saw the almost-destroyed plaster, the missing fixtures, and the cracked toilet filled with black water. "Needs a little spit-shine in here, too."

"It might save you time if I describe the rooms that *don't* need work."

"Which ones?"

"None of them, Jim. Absolutely none of them. This place is a disaster. That's why it's only $2,500."

Jim slapped the door leading into the kitchen with his palm. The *thwock* of the impact sent more plaster to the floor. "It's perfect. I'll take it."

Brad's mouth hung open. "Are you serious?"

"Yeah. Should I just get my checkbook and pay for it now? How much time do you need to get the paperwork ready?"

After a few minutes of discussion over the logistics, Brad walked out the front door, shaking his head in disbelief. "I'll give you a minute before I come back to lock it up," he shouted.

Feeling good about himself, Jim pulled his phone out of his pocket and dialed Pete Stabone.

"Pete!"

"Jim! How was Austria?"

"Real good. Guess where I'm calling from?"

"I hate these games, Jim."

"Let's just call it, 'home base.'"

The term confused Pete. "I don't think I get it. That's not something we've said in the past, Jim. Where are you? At the hotel?"

"Nope, I'm not. I'm in a house that I'm about to buy."

There was a pause. "For what?"

"Pete, her name is Victoria Hewitt."

"The vampire?"

"That's her. It was her in the video. I've found her, Pete. The search is over."

"That's great! Have you talked to her or anything? What's the plan?"

Jim walked across the kitchen and peeked at the backyard through the broken panes of the window. "Nope, I'm not going to talk to her."

"What do you mean? What are you going to do? Why did you buy a house?"

"It's brilliant, really. Think about it, Pete; she's not going to come peacefully. There's just no chance of that happening. If I take her to the hotel to talk things over, she'll make a big stink. I'll attract a lot of unwanted attention, and this whole thing could fall apart. Instead, I bought a house just down the road from her place, and I can whisk her over here to deal with her."

"But…she's still going to fight it."

"Yeah, but we have privacy here. I haven't looked at the basement, but maybe I can just put her down there."

On the other end of the line, Pete placed his hand over his face. "Jim, you're not serious."

"What?"

"You're talking about kidnapping a teenage girl and holding her in the basement of some house you just bought? Are you out of your mind?"

The reaction annoyed Jim. "First, she's not a 'teenage girl.' She just looks like one. This is a powerful, dangerous creature. You saw what that thing did to the car in the video, right? She has to be dealt with. And second, what did you *think* we were going to do? Ask her to come with us and leave if she told us to get lost?"

"No, but… I don't know. I wasn't expecting you to go this far."

"It's not going far. It's being sensible and planning for the situation. She is dangerous, she can hurt people, and I'm going to make sure she can't. This monster needs to be neutralized before anything else can happen."

"How did you even buy this house?"

Jim laughed. "She lives in a really lousy neighborhood.

There are houses around here for under three grand. I just wrote them a check."

"You seriously bought a house? What are you going to do with it after the fact?"

"Who cares? Burn it down."

"So, you're just willing to throw away three thousand dollars?"

Jim heard a *crack* under his feet as he walked across the kitchen. He spun to see another board in the floor broken from supporting the weight of an average man. "Let's imagine for a moment that we've got the President of the United States standing here. We've done all the research, gathered all the evidence, and we have a killer game plan for him. Everything we need is right there, except, you know, the monster. You don't think that's worth three grand? I'd pay twenty thousand dollars to have the assurance that we're going to get this to the finish line. I've spent so much of my time tracking down this vampire and months here in Milwaukee trying to locate her. I'm taking every possible precaution so that I can bring her in, keep her here, and get her into the right hands. I'll pay whatever it takes to make that a reality."

"Jim, I think you need to lie down. I wanted you to get excited about this, but you're still talking about kidnapping another being. This isn't like the zombie thing where you were using bodies that were dead anyway. This is somebody with a life and friends and family…"

"Pete, knock it off. Knock it off right now. This is not a human being. This is not somebody who has a bunch of family. It's not an American citizen, even. This is a foreign supernatural creature who poses a threat—a very real and recorded threat—to the public at large. She can be instrumental in saving lives if we can harness her power and train her to fight *for* us."

"And what if you can't? What if you get all this way, and she refuses? What then? Are you just going to give up? What happens if you do all this and it still doesn't work?"

There was a long pause.

"Pete, my career is on the line. I don't care what happens—she's *going* to work with me, whether she likes it or not. Failure is not an option. I'll talk to you later."

He hung up the phone and stuffed it back into his pocket. *Doesn't matter who supports me and who doesn't. I'll show them all. I'll bring this one in. This time, nobody will be laughing at me. I'll be the one who brought the US government a vampire on a silver platter. All I have to do is get her here.*

CHAPTER ELEVEN

Alexis stared into the bathroom mirror as other girls washed their hands and fixed their makeup. The chatter was endless.

"It's so cold in here!"

"I know! Like, it's getting to be summer outside, and I'm all bundled up in long sleeves and jeans."

Alexis shook her head, trying not to look too annoyed. *What did you think was going to happen at an ice rink, girls?* But her mind was preoccupied with other thoughts.

Like the last time she had gone ice skating.

The awkwardness. The feeling that something wasn't quite right. And of course, the realization later on that she was ice skating with a Sanguinarian who wanted to consume her flesh.

The thought sent a chill racing down her spine, and her skin pricked with goosebumps. She shuddered and rubbed her bare arms.

"See?" One of the other girls pointed at her. "This one's already shivering, and we're not even out on the ice yet!"

"No, it's…" Alexis let her voice trail off. *What's the point of explaining it to these airheads? They wouldn't know what I was talking about anyway.*

Once she felt prepared, Alexis walked out of the bathroom and into the lobby of the Pettit Center. Charlie was waiting for her with a smile plastered on his face. He had a pair of skates tied together by the laces hanging around his neck. "What do you think of my new necklace? Nice, right?"

"Looks a little bulky for you."

"Darn. I was going for 'masculine.' I figured bulky was good."

The two of them laughed. For Alexis, dating Charlie was easy. He was fun and quirky, and he seemed to really enjoy being around her. It was so refreshing, she almost didn't know how to handle it most of the time.

"I didn't get your skates just because I don't know what size you wear." Charlie pointed to the rental counter. "But they know you're coming. You're all paid up."

"Thanks." She smiled at him and headed to the rental counter, returning moments later with a pair of skates slung over her shoulder.

"You wear it better." Charlie winked.

"Guys are supposed to *buy* jewelry for the girls, not rent it."

Charlie let out a belly laugh as he pulled open the heavy metal door leading to the rink area. A blast of cold air hit them in the face.

As they sat on the bench to strap the skates to their feet, Charlie exhaled deeply.

"You okay?" Alexis paused and glanced at him.

"Yeah. I just… I have a confession to make."

Great. You're actually a bloodthirsty vampire, too. What could it be? Am I just attracting the weirdos?

"I've never gone ice skating before."

"Oh." Although she hadn't really been worried that he was really a Sang, she was relieved that the confession was something so minor. "Well, that's okay. It's a lot of fun. Don't stress about it. The key is to be relaxed."

Charlie had his skates tied and ready to go, so he sat up straight on the bench and watched the other skaters fly by. "What happens if I fall?"

Alexis giggled. "It's not like you're falling from twenty feet in the air. Have you ever fallen before? Put your hands out, and you'll be fine. Look, little kids are out there, flopping all over the place."

Charlie shook his head. "Well, sure they are. They have a shorter distance to fall." Alexis laughed at the notion. "Plus, they have young bones. Kids can fall all they want, and they never get hurt."

She stood up and took him by the hand. "Come on. Let's get out there. The skates are on, so it's too late for you to back out."

Reluctantly, Charlie stood up from the bench and waddled over the rubber mats leading to the ice rink. When his feet hit the ice, they slipped. He held his breath and pulled his feet under his body, trying to look comfortable even though it was obvious he wasn't.

"Well, now, this is an odd feeling." Alexis spun and glided backward in front of the stumbling boy.

"What?"

"I'm your classic self-conscious teenage girl. You're the

confident, relaxed, popular boy. Yet, right now, I'm the confident and relaxed one, and you couldn't look more out of your element."

Charlie awkwardly skidded to the rail at the edge of the rink and clutched at it with both arms. As he touched it, his feet shot out in front of his body, and he fell to the ice. Alexis laughed.

"Gee, thanks for the concern!" He shot her a playfully-annoyed look.

She skated to his side and went down on one knee. "Oh, you're fine. Is your tailbone broken?"

"It could be bruised!" His voice took on a sarcastic tone. "I could have shattered my pelvis, and you're sitting there laughing at me!"

"I'm getting anxious. While you're trying to get to your feet, I'm going to go do a lap. Watch how it's done!" She skated off to join the circle of skaters doing laps around the rink. As she moved effortlessly across the ice, she smiled. *This is a far cry from the last time. Maybe I'm not holding hands with him as we skate side by side, but we're laughing and having fun!*

Halfway around the rink, a blond boy sidled up to her on the ice, matching her speed. "Hey."

"Hey."

"You're really good on the ice."

"Thanks." *This is weird.*

"I'm Jake. What's your name?"

"Alexis." *Why is he talking to me?*

"You come to the Pettit a lot?"

"Well, this is the first time I've been here with my boyfriend."

Jake raised his eyebrows. "Oh, you're here with somebody?"

Alexis pointed to the handsome young man clinging to the rail, trying desperately not to fall down. "Yeah. That one's mine."

The intruding boy laughed it off. "You mean that guy who looks like he's terrified of getting anywhere near the ice? Real winner there."

She shot him an annoyed look. "Hey, you know what? That guy is awesome, and he treats me well. Best of all, he doesn't come across like he's full of himself. I'll take that over whatever you are any day of the week. Leave me alone."

"*Pff.*" Jake skated away, and Alexis picked up the pace to return to her boyfriend.

When Charlie saw her coming around the bend, he let go of the rail and turned to join her. "If you promise to go slow, I'll join you for this lap."

"I believe in you!" She smiled at him.

Charlie was a natural athlete, but not on the ice. Despite being one of the leaders of the wrestling team at Clear Lake High School, and generally coordinated, he looked as uncoordinated as anyone possibly could while skating.

Alexis couldn't help but laugh at his form. "You look like Frankenstein!"

"What?" Charlie's upper body swayed as he tried to move forward.

"You need to relax. Bend your knees a little. Let your hips do the work. You're keeping your legs stiff, and it's making you work twice as hard to keep going. Watch me."

Alexis spun in front of him and extended her hands. Charlie took them, and she nodded at her legs, skating backward and pulling him along.

Charlie shook his head. "You make it look effortless. I'm taking to this like a duck to auto repair."

"That's the most ridiculous analogy I've ever heard."

"Hey, it fits! I've never felt so unnatural."

"That's just because you need to relax. Look at me." She bent toward him, and the two locked eyes. Alexis wore a permanent smirk as she pulled him along, and he stared deeply into her eyes, falling harder for her with every sway.

Then he fell even harder—literally.

He grunted when his body flopped onto the ice like a pancake. Alexis shrieked, but muffled it with laughter. "Are you okay?"

Just as he sat up and tried to regain his bearings, Jake sped past again, shaking his head. Alexis gave him a mean look while she helped Charlie onto his feet.

"You know that guy?" Charlie appeared confused.

"No. He's just some jerk that skated over to me and started hitting on me while I was skating before."

"I know. I saw."

Alexis returned to her spot in front of Charlie, facing him while she pulled him along the ice. "You know what? If this is how we have to skate, then this is how we have to skate today. I'm fine with it."

"Well, I certainly like the view."

The comment made her blush. "So, you didn't like seeing that guy talking to me?"

He shrugged. "A guy can tell when another guy is trying

to hit on his girlfriend." He paused and looked at the rival boy. "Besides, he seems like an attractive dude, and he is clearly better on skates than me."

"That's not everything." She tilted her head sympathetically. *He's feeling vulnerable. He's just as self-conscious as me after all!* "The guy's a total jerk, and he obviously knows he's good-looking. That's the worst kind. I'd rather have someone who makes me laugh."

Charlie looked nervously at his legs, which refused to loosen up, no matter what he did. "Well, if laughing is what attracts you, I guess we're doing the right activity!"

"That's not what I mean! I didn't bring you here to laugh at you. I thought it would be fun. And you know what? I'm having a blast, even if I have to drag you across the ice."

He smiled at her. "I'm glad you're having a good time."

"I totally am! You make me laugh in other ways too, and besides, you're cuter than that guy."

Charlie took a deep, cleansing breath. Hearing her say that gave him a renewed sense of confidence, and gradually his knees relaxed.

"Look at you!" Alexis nodded at his legs. "Now you're getting it. Just keep doing what you're doing."

"So this is what you meant. This is a lot easier than what I was doing before."

"Right, that's what I was trying to tell you!"

Alexis swung around to his side and held one of his hands, leading him rather than pulling him. They took a few more laps around the rink, smiling and laughing as they moved along.

"You know, there's something I've wanted to say to you." The smile fell from Charlie's face.

"What's that?"

He took a longer-than-comfortable pause, which gave Alexis time to overthink whatever he was about to say.

What is it? Is he breaking up with me? Does he not think we're going to last? Did he hate that I was laughing at him before? Oh, man, that's it, isn't it? I knew this was too good to be true.

"I just...never mind. I forgot what it was. Slipped my mind."

"Seriously?" The knot in Alexis' stomach tightened.

"Yeah. I guess with all these people here, and I'm so focused on not falling on my butt again in front you... Just bounced out of my head. I'll get it back later, I'm sure."

Great. Now I can sweat about it for a lot longer. That's good.

The two of them skated for a while, enjoying them-selves, even if Charlie's reluctance to talk about what was on his mind hung in the air awkwardly. Both of them, however, refused to address it any further.

CHAPTER TWELVE

"Are you sure you're up for this?"

Vickie paused from stuffing a pair of jeans into her duffel bag and spun to see Alexis standing in the door of her bedroom. "What, you think this is a bad idea?"

Alexis crossed her arms and leaned against the frame. "You don't have to do this."

Vickie resumed packing. "I have been spending way too much time trying to avoid being a vampire that I haven't been able to enjoy being a human." She grabbed her pink cross-country sweatshirt. "How cold do you think it'll be tonight?"

"Cold enough for a sweatshirt." Alexis sighed. "I just don't want anything bad to happen to you. Or anyone else, for that matter."

"To tell you the truth, I feel a little better tonight." Vickie sat down on the edge of her bed and rested her arm on the duffel bag. "Besides, I want to know what all the fuss is about. All I've heard about during the last few months is how awesome the last night of school is. Todd Benson said the other day that the last night celebration was the only reason he came to school."

"It's just so different from the rest of the year." Alexis giggled as she walked into the room and sat down next to her. "There's a vibe in the parking lot, you know? A bunch of students from all classes, hanging out in the shadow of the school building. Some of them fall asleep. Oh, I didn't mention that. Do not fall asleep!"

The advice confused Vickie. "Why would I fall asleep? Isn't the whole point of the last night supposed to be staying up all night? Partying in the parking lot?"

"Yeah, but come on, not everyone is cut out for all-nighters. There are usually a handful of students who will do their best to stay up but nod off just enough that they won't know what's going on. Then we pounce."

"Pounce?" Vickie bent over to grab her shoes from under the bed.

"Yeah. It depends on the kid and if they're a jerk or whatever. Also depends who's around. But they'll get pranked for sure."

"What kinds of pranks happen at this thing?"

Alexis laughed. "Last year, one guy got his car covered in shaving cream. That stuff is really hard to clean off once it dries! Another guy had a mustache drawn on his face with permanent marker. Like, it's always harmless little things, but it's just tradition. But maybe your instincts will kick in if they know something's about to happen while you're sleeping. I wouldn't chance it."

Vickie placed her hand on her stomach. "I don't know what's going on anymore. I still feel weird, but for some reason, I feel less pain than normal."

"You think whatever threat that's been hanging around might have gone away?"

"I doubt it. Of course, maybe some group was after me and they all died in a plane crash, so the threat is over." She slipped on her shoes. "Then again, maybe my body is just having mercy on me and giving me a break. Either way, I'll take whatever I can get."

There was a knock on the door.

"Hey, Dad." Alexis stood up. "Just giving Vickie the rundown of the last night."

He nodded. "Oh, really? I'll bet. Sit back down, I want to talk to you both about this."

Alexis fought the urge to obnoxiously roll her eyes as she sat back down on the bed.

Her father stepped in closer. "I have no problem with the both of you going to the last night. It's a school tradition, and it's largely innocent fun. But it is also a group of high school kids who are not supervised staying up all night. I need you both to be responsible."

His daughter shrugged. "I'm sure most of it is just going to be chilling in the parking lot, swapping stories, playing games…stuff like that. I went last year, and there wasn't any drinking or anything like you might worry about."

"Well, I trust you both. Just please be on your best behavior. Vickie, how are you feeling?"

"I'm okay." She stood and zipped her duffel bag. "It comes and goes. I think it's going to be fine tonight."

"I'm a little wary of you going since you've had so many problems lately."

"I was asking her the same thing, Dad."

"Both of you can relax," Vickie urged. "I know myself. I

have very good control of my instincts. I won't accidentally kill anybody or break anything. It'll be fun tonight. If I sense anything going wrong, I'll make sure I don't go crazy."

"What are you going to do all night, Dad? Anything fun? Call your new girlfriend?"

Craig shook his head. "No, it'll be a quiet one around here. Hey, it's still a weeknight. I'll probably just enjoy having the TV to myself for the whole night."

He took them to the school and started to turn into the parking lot when Alexis stopped him. "Dad, wait!"

He slammed on the brakes. "What? What's going on?"

"You can't go into the lot. Drop us off here."

"Seriously?"

"Tonight is about freedom and enjoying ourselves as young adults. Any parents who drop off their kids do that up here by the street."

Craig looked at Vickie in the rearview mirror, rolled his eyes, and pulled the car to the sidewalk. "Be careful, be safe, have fun."

Alexis leaned over and kissed her father on the cheek before pushing open the passenger-side door, dragging her bag behind her. "Love you!"

"Love you, too. Vickie, are you getting out?"

Vickie felt a little tightness in her stomach, but she did her best to ignore it. "Yep. I'm going. Thanks for the ride."

"You got it. Be safe out there. Enjoy being a teenager for the night."

She smiled at him before getting out of the car and slamming the door behind her. Vickie stood next to Alexis. "Well? Do we just go in?"

"Follow me." Alexis led Vickie to the entrance to the parking lot, which dipped sharply down from the street level. From their vantage point, they could see the whole parking lot, and it was bustling with activity. A few packs of students were scattered around the lot. A good handful of them huddled around a fire surrounded by lawn chairs in the far corner, near the entrance to the track. Alexis pointed at the fire. "There's the headquarters for the night. We'll start by hanging out there. We can leave our bags there and get a feel for who's all here."

The two girls carefully walked down the steep slope of the parking lot entrance. A sharp wind blew through, causing Alexis to shiver. "Brrrr! A little colder than last year."

"Why is that?" Vickie shook her head. "If it was warmer last year, why wouldn't it be warmer this year?"

"Still not used to living in Wisconsin, hey?" Alexis laughed. "Come on. It could be ninety degrees tomorrow morning, or we could get a foot of snow. In this part of the world, either of those makes sense in May."

The girls approached the group by the fire, who greeted them. Vickie was taken aback by how welcoming everyone was. She followed Alexis off to the side, where a pile of duffel bags rested at the edge of the pavement.

"This is weird," Vickie commented.

"Why?"

"Because everyone is being so nice! High school the past year has been, like, the most cutthroat environment I've ever been in. At least, without anyone actually trying to kill each other. Backstabbing, constant judgment... Why is everyone being so cool right now?"

Alexis shrugged. "That's the last night for you. Think of the school year as some kind of battle. We went to war together for the last nine months. This night is a celebration and appreciation of each other, so everyone is nice to everybody else since we were all in it together. For this night, everyone is just...*cool* with everyone else. It's a nice change of pace."

"I'll say. There are some popular kids around that fire, and they greeted me like I'm not the weird new girl or the girl who botched the question in Physical Science last week."

Alexis patted her on the shoulder. "So then, tonight should be just what you need. Enjoy it."

A tall, burly football player stood at a folding table that held a few bottles of punch and a case of bottled water. As the girls approached to get something to drink, he shook his head. "None of the good stuff here tonight."

"He means beer." Alexis nudged Vickie with her elbow.

"Why not?" Vickie asked him.

"You drink?" He seemed surprised that a sophomore girl would ask.

"No, it's not that. I'm just surprised. There's no supervision. It feels like this would be the perfect time for a bunch of idiots to bring in a keg."

The boy scoffed at the idea. "First of all, we might be unsupervised, but it's still a parking lot. We're not that stupid. Cops will come rolling through here once in a while tonight to make sure we're not doing anything too stupid. Second, the last night is one of the few fun things we get to do at Clear Lake that everyone is cool with. If word got out that we brought beer, that would be the end of it."

Vickie grabbed a bottle of water, and the girls walked over to the fire. Alexis looked at the four girls huddled under blankets and waved politely at them. "Anyone fall asleep yet? It's only 9:30, but last year there was a sleeper already by now."

A redheaded girl giggled. "Yeah, Tim Kveen was caught dozing about twenty minutes ago. He wasn't fully asleep, but enough."

"What'd they do to him?"

They pointed at two bags that were set apart from the rest of the pile. "Padlocked his bag and his backpack together, then connected a few more padlocks to it. It's going to take him forever to get them off if he wants a change of clothes or his books!"

Everyone laughed, and Vickie settled into a chair, cautiously enjoying the little bit of freedom she was having. For the first time since she got to Clear Lake High School, she was surrounded by a bunch of other kids and wasn't feeling so self-conscious. For once, it was a community that seemed to enjoy each other's company, rather than a bunch of kids who didn't want anything to do with her.

For the next two hours, Alexis and Vickie sat around the fire, telling stories about what had happened over the past year, and listening to the gossip about faculty members supposedly engaging in romantic liaisons, stories of Principal Goede's allegedly checkered past, and legends of what used to happen during last night celebrations of the past.

Still, despite the fun, welcoming environment, Vickie was wary of her stomach. Her fangs weren't poking out, but she was just uncomfortable enough that she found her mind drifting away from the conversations while she tried to figure out if there indeed was a threat nearby, or if this was the new normal.

Meanwhile, back at the hotel, Jim Trembo changed into an all-black outfit, hoping the darkness would camouflage him.

CHAPTER THIRTEEN

*H*ow *Much Will You Give Me?* was another game certain members of the student body enjoyed playing during the last night. Vickie had not witnessed it before, and the concept confused her.

It all started when Steve Molenda approached the girls around the fire with a devilish smile on his face. He was flanked by two of his buddies, who were already laughing.

"All right, girls, how much will you give me if I streak?"

Vickie shot Alexis a confused look. Alexis leaned in. "'Streak' means run around naked."

A horrified look washed over Vickie's face. "Ugh! On purpose?"

Steve rolled his eyes. "Don't be such a prude. Come on, how much will you give me?"

Vickie looked at Alexis. "What is going on? Why is he asking this?"

"Some of the stupider guys do that on nights like these. They come up with something really stupid, and then they try to outdo each other to see who can be stupider. Usually it's for money, so they try to find the most ridiculous things they can do and see if they can raise the most money." She looked at Steve. "I'll throw in five bucks."

"Alexis!" Vickie's mouth hung agape. "You want to see him naked? What would Charlie say?"

"First of all, Charlie's not here. Second, streaking isn't about getting to see anybody naked. It's about the stunt."

"Yeah," Steve chimed in. "I'm not going to, like, drop trou right here by the fire! I'll go strip behind a car or something. Nobody's getting an up-close view. Come on, that's good for a couple bucks, right?"

Other girls jumped in, and soon Steve had secured enough bids to total twenty dollars. Once all the bids were in, he agreed to do it. Many of the kids who had scattered around the parking lot had now congregated by the fire, around twenty or so students.

Steve ran his fingers through his shaggy blond hair and scanned the parking lot. "Okay, I'm going to go behind that green truck. I'm leaving my stuff there, and if so much as a sock has been moved by the time I get back, I'm going to bust heads."

"Where are you running to?" one of the girls asked.

"Yeah, it only counts if you're going to go somewhere public, like the Pick 'n Save parking lot." One of his buddies slapped him on the back, and the group laughed.

"How about I do a lap around the school building?"

The crowd cheered their approval, and Steve jogged over to the green truck. Running a lap around the school building meant that Steve would be running in front of the school, which would be on the sidewalk next to a major road. Even at midnight, there would still be the occasional car driving past.

"I'm keeping my shoes and socks on, though!" he shouted from the truck. The group laughed.

Vickie held her hand over her mouth. "I can't believe he's doing this."

"Relax, you won't see anything." Alexis tapped her on the shoulder. "It's just to be stupid. He's so far away, all you're going to be able to see is skin."

To the cheers coming from the far end of the parking lot, Steve Molenda took off running behind the school. Just as Alexis had predicted, nobody could see anything other than the glow of his pale skin shining under the occasional overhead light.

He disappeared into the shadows, turning the corner to head up to the street as various kids discussed openly whether he would emerge from the other side of the school building.

"Think he'll actually do it?"

"I'm not going up there to check!"

"I bet he bailed. He's probably still in the shadows, too chicken to run out."

"Maybe he got caught. What if a cop drove past?"

"They *are* due to show up any time now."

"Wait, there he is!"

Applause and hollers from the crowd greeted Steve as he rounded the corner and ran down the entrance to the parking lot, turning immediately to his left to make a beeline for the green truck.

One guy shook his head. "I've never been more thankful for a large parking lot at this school. I'm so glad he's all the way over there right now." The comment got laughs.

Minutes later, a panting and fully dressed Steve Molenda reappeared, to one more chorus of applause. "Thank you, thank you." He took a bow as he extended his hand out to collect his winnings.

"Nobody saw you?"

He shrugged. "A couple cars drove past, but I'm sure they were moving so fast, they didn't realize there was a naked guy running down the sidewalk."

Three other guys stepped forward. "All right, we're going to hop the fence and run the track naked!" Vickie only knew the boys as Matt, Paul, and Dan. They were a weird group of guys who were generally liked.

Soon, they had collected enough money that they felt the pursuit was worth it. The crowd moved to the entrance to the track and football field, which was gated and locked.

"You're not stripping down here, are you?" Steve wanted to confirm. "If so, I'm running the other direction!"

"No," Matt replied. "I'm not jumping any fences naked. We'll get over there, then go to the far side of the track. At least it's dark over there."

"All right, get to work!"

The boys climbed the chain-link fence and ran across the football field, laughing obnoxiously. The rest of the group pressed against the fence.

"They're crazy."

"We should find a way to keep them stuck on the track all night."

"It's pretty dark over there. We might not even see them."

"I hope we don't. But here they come!"

The boys' pale skin proved their nakedness as they rounded the track in just their shoes. The crowd laughed at them, and they waved at the rest of the group as they ran wildly, their limbs flailing.

Vickie was once again disgusted. "Boy, I didn't realize there would be so much nudity at this thing."

"Some years are nakeder than others," a boy commented to her, making up a word to describe the situation.

About an hour later, the group had resumed regular activities. Everyone was fully clothed again, and the adrenaline of the streaking activities had worn off. In its place was a general sense of fatigue and boredom.

The first two to fall asleep were Angie Mull and Tyler Nix, who sat on opposite sides of the fire, snoring.

The realization that two people had fallen asleep sent a shockwave of renewed energy through the group. A few of the guys hung back, plotting the prank they were going to pull on each of them.

Alexis waved Vickie over, trying to include her in the fun, and hoping to keep her awake. They leaned in to hear what the plans were.

"Check it out." One guy pointed to a couple of parking spaces. "Angie and Tyler parked right next to each other. It's like it was meant to be!"

"What was?" Vickie asked. "What is the plan?"

"We were going to encase Tyler's car in plastic wrap, but since Angie's car is there too, we're going to do both of them...*together*."

The pranksters laughed and one of them ran to his car,

returning with a grocery bag full of rolls of plastic wrap. Once they all assembled by the two cars, they paused.

"I don't know," one said. "I think they're parked too far apart."

"How heavy is a car? Maybe we can just move it?"

Alexis grabbed Vickie by the arm and pulled her aside. "How are you feeling?"

"Fine, I guess."

"Can you tap into your powers?"

Vickie took a deep breath. "I've got control over them right now. Why?" Alexis whispered a plan in her ear, and Vickie nodded. "Yeah, we can do that."

They returned to the group as they were still discussing what to do. "A car isn't that heavy," Alexis announced. "Just put a few people on one end of the car and move it over, then go to the other end and slide it over. With enough people, it should be easy."

They agreed to give it a shot, and Alexis placed Vickie strategically in the middle of the group. Five kids lifted the bumper of Angie's two-door coupe, and Vickie felt her fangs poke the insides of her lips as she easily hoisted the car, shouldering nearly all the weight.

The other guys laughed at how light the car felt. "This sure is a lot easier with everybody doing it!"

They slid the car against the other one.

"Oh, man, this is going to be so good!" One of the guys rubbed his hands together. "They can't even get into their cars this way!"

The realization hit the crowd, and they erupted in laughter. Tyler had backed into his parking space, and Angie had parked forward in hers. Because of the way they were parked, moving their cars together had placed their driver's side doors against each other.

The kids passed out rolls of plastic wrap and yanked them out of their boxes. With almost a military level efficiency, the group systematically passed the rolls back and forth, encasing the two cars in a thick layer of plastic wrap both horizontally and vertically.

When they were finished, they all stood back to admire their handiwork. "This is the greatest thing I've ever done in my life," Steve Molenda commented.

"Greater than running around the school naked, Steve?" one guy shouted.

He laughed. "It's been a big night for me!"

The two victims of the plastic wrap prank did not wake up for another hour. In the meantime, two police officers visited the lot to check on the group, and they were satisfied with what they saw. The fire was contained in a fire pit, and everyone appeared to be sober and not too loud or unruly.

The two officers laughed at the sight of the two shrink-wrapped cars.

Once they left, a few of the guys high-fived each other, satisfied that they were safe.

When the victims woke up, they grumbled at the sight of their cars wrapped together so tight. "My mom is going to kill me!" Angie moaned.

Tyler, however, shrugged his shoulders and laughed it off. "This is stupid. I'll have to get a knife or something." He poked at the layers of plastic, which had to be an inch thick. "Good grief. This is going to take me like an hour."

"It took us a while too, man!" a boy joked. "Shoot, we all nearly threw out our backs moving the cars together!"

Alexis rolled her eyes at Vickie, who laughed. They knew who had done all the heavy lifting, but it was fine. They let the boys talk.

Even though she was enjoying herself, Vickie's instincts were starting to grow stronger. She found herself daydreaming about what could possibly occur that evening that would trip her up.

She didn't know it, but Jim Trembo was twenty minutes away from the school, heading toward it in his car.

CHAPTER FOURTEEN

When the last night hit 3:00AM, the crowd was starting to lose their energy.

Nobody had the will to pull any more pranks. Even the wildest of the bunch had run out of steam. Some of the students had tapped out, falling asleep in their chairs around the fire, or sprawled out on the grass next to the parking lot. Some of the kids were not asleep but had zoned out completely, staring blankly into the fire and watching the flames dance.

Alexis and Vickie were slowing down, but they were still awake. Alexis stared at the clear night sky, squinting at the bright moon. "What a beautiful night."

"Perfect night for this," another girl commented. Heads nodded in agreement around the fire.

"It's too calm," Steve said. "At least with crummy weather, there's energy around here. This party is dying hard."

"Why aren't there more people here?" Vickie asked him.

"There are, what, twenty people? The school has almost a thousand kids."

"They're weak." Steve laughed. "Naw, it's just one of those things you either think is really cool or really stupid. Some people had to work. Others are worried about their exam scores if they have tests yet to take. All depends. I think that's what's fun about the last night. It's never predictable."

"Kind of like *The Breakfast Club*." Alexis smiled.

"The what?" Vickie closed one eye, trying to think of the reference.

"*The Breakfast Club* was a movie in the eighties where a group of kids have to spend their Saturday in detention, but it's a weird mixed bag of students from different parts of the social circle. What made it interesting was how they interacted with each other. They didn't hang out before then, so they learned about themselves along the way. Like, I haven't ever hung out with Steve over there, but now I know he's a dude who likes to run around naked."

Steve roared with laughter. "Let's not go that far! I like to make money, girl. That's all. And now I know you're a bit of a jerk!"

She laughed in response. Vickie was confused by the exchange, but she laughed along with them. After Steve got up from the fire, she leaned over to Alexis. "What was that?"

"What?"

"You were flirting with him."

"No, I wasn't! I have a boyfriend!"

"Yeah, but he's not here."

"So? Neither is yours."

"Yeah, but I'm wishing he was. I haven't seen Eric much during the last few weeks."

Alexis nodded. "Yeah, he's a big-time study guy. He'll put in hours of work to get good grades. I always tell him he doesn't have to. He's one of the smartest kids in school. There's no need to triple-check your work all the time! Is that why he's not here?"

"Yep. I almost begged him to come because we hadn't spent any good time together in forever. I thought it would be nice if the two of us got to hang out, but he insisted he had to study."

"Yeah, I'm not surprised. That's Eric for you. That kid needs to trust his head; he's studying stuff he already knows. I bet he would ace most of his exams just from what he remembered from class. Would save him a lot of trouble."

Vickie pulled her knees to her chest. "What about Charlie? What's he doing tonight?"

"He had to work until, like, 11:00." Alexis shook her head in disappointment. "He said he would probably be so tired from work that he would come out and get pranked before midnight. I didn't blame him. Wish he was here, though."

"Sitting by a fire under the full moon seems really romantic. It *is* romantic, right?" Vickie still struggled with the basics of teen romance in the 21st century.

"Yes, it's romantic." Alexis giggled. "If you say it's romantic, then it's romantic. But yeah, most girls would like that."

The two of them sat in silence for a while, thinking about their boyfriends and how badly they wished the two boys were there. It bummed them both out, but they tried to keep a happy face.

Then again, given the time of the night, nobody had much of a happy face.

Steve Molenda, however, was there to save the day again. "Okay, crew! Let's huddle up!" The girls spun in their chairs to see him twirling a football on his finger.

"Really, Steve?" Alexis rolled her eyes. "I can barely keep my eyes open as it is. Now we're supposed to get up and run around?"

Steve hopped in place on his heels. "Hey, that's how you stay awake, folks! Get your blood pumping! The reason we're all falling asleep is that we're sitting around doing nothing. It's our own fault. Let's go, gang! I want to pick teams."

About a dozen other kids slowly dragged themselves from their chairs or their blankets on the grass to join in. Two other guys were jogging in place, getting their energy up, but the rest were moving slower than molasses.

Once they picked teams, the group split in two and moved to opposite sides of the parking lot. Steve shouted directions. "Okay, the end zones are from this car down to Tyler's car on the other end. Everyone gets four downs or it's a turnover. Kickoffs will just be thrown. Wave your hand when you're ready!"

Soon, the ball was in the air and the kids were running around, starting to warm up their bodies and their minds for a second wind that evening.

Fortunately for Vickie, she had watched a lot of American football in the Watson house, thanks to Craig's undying love for the Green Bay Packers. During the first few games of the season, she had been enraptured, absorbing every rule and every step of the game, and asking questions whenever they popped into her head.

So when the game began, Vickie was confident. She knew that she could play a good game of football because she knew what to do.

Unfortunately, that did not translate to actually being able to play the game.

Alexis and Vickie found themselves on opposite teams, and they matched up on offense and defense. Vickie's team had the ball first and she immediately broke away from Alexis, waving her arm to signal that she was open. The quarterback, a very athletic boy named Tony, launched a perfect spiral through the air toward her.

As the ball came flying down, Vickie suddenly realized she didn't know how to catch a football. The ball dropped into her hands, but she bobbled the catch and dropped it for an incomplete pass.

Alexis laughed. "Hey, you better not be using your powers, girl. That's cheating!"

"Shut up, I'm not. It just feels like I'm using my powers because you're that slow!"

The girls laughed as they jogged back to their respective huddles. Tony pulled Vickie aside. "Hey, break free again, but stay closer this time. We'll cut the field in half. Everyone else, go out and look like you're supposed to catch the ball. We'll fool 'em."

The team broke the huddle and hiked the ball. The defender targeting the quarterback bounced in place, counting out loud to five, hoping to have a chance to tag him before he threw the ball.

Once again, Vickie left Alexis in her dust, cutting to her left to be wide open. Tony threw a dart of a pass at her, and once again, it hit her in the hands. Once again, she dropped the pass.

A few of the players on her team groaned in disappointment. Vickie grew more frustrated and more embarrassed with each play.

Steve Molenda, seeing her turning red even in the dark, jogged over to her and called for a time out.

"Vickie, check it out." He held out his hands, bringing the tips of his thumbs together and the tips of his fingers together to form a diamond shape with his hands. "Make this shape." Vickie lifted her hands and copied him. "If you do this with your hands when you're going for a catch, you'll hold onto it. That ball can't make it through the diamond. Just close your hands around the ball, then."

Vickie nodded and smiled back at him. "Thanks for the help. I appreciate it. I'll give it a shot."

He patted her on the shoulder and jogged back to his huddle. "All right, Wildcats, let's get a pick and take it to the house."

That was really nice of him. And he's not even on my team! On the next play, Vickie broke free again. To the frustration of the rest of the team, Tony once again tried to pass it to her, hoping that the impromptu lesson from Steve would be enough to transform her game.

Unfortunately, just as the ball was reaching her hands, her stomach tightened in pain on her. She doubled over, trying not to grunt or let on that she was in serious pain. The ball dropped to the ground.

"All right! Turnover on downs!" Steve clapped his hands

and jogged over to retrieve the ball.

Alexis ran to Vickie. "You okay?"

"I'm fine."

"No, you're not. I can tell when you're hiding it. Your instincts are flaring up, aren't they?"

"You want to keep it down?" Vickie looked around in panic. "I don't need anyone else knowing about me."

"You're fine. But are your senses being tripped? What are you feeling? How are you feeling it? Talk to me."

Vickie rubbed her stomach. "Now isn't the time. Let's just play some football and have fun."

Next door, Jim Trembo pulled into the parking lot of the grocery store and parked his car. He leaned forward and peered through the bushes separating the parking lot of the store from the parking lot of the school. Seeing the glow of the fire coming from the far end of the parking lot, he smiled.

Perfect. They're still going, and I know she's there. That was why I followed her here tonight. This is it. This is the night I get my hands on that vampire girl.

Back in the school parking lot, Vickie finished the rest of the game, moving at half the speed she had started with. Her mind began to race, and her stomach twisted so hard, she worried that she was going to throw up. *Great, you're already embarrassed because you can't catch a football. Now you're going to puke in front of everyone? That's really attractive, Vickie. Way to endear yourself to the rest of the student body.*

Despite her frustration, she couldn't will her senses to leave her alone. There was something bad, and it was very close to her.

CHAPTER FIFTEEN

The football game petered out rather suddenly. Steve appeared disappointed when it was clear that nobody wanted to keep going.

"You guys need to go next door and get some energy drinks in your system or something! We still have a few more hours until school starts!"

The group let out a collective groan.

Vickie stepped away from the group with Alexis at her side. "He's right. Maybe we need to jump over to the supermarket."

"What do you need?"

"Something. Anything. I don't know what, but I'm getting hungry and anxious, and maybe there's some food that we can buy that will calm me down, or at least help me be a little more comfortable."

Alexis nodded. "Let's do it, but let's sneak away. I don't want anybody following us."

They began walking across the parking lot, and Steve

ran up behind them. "Hey, wait up! You're going to Pick 'n Save?"

Shoot. He's going to want to come along. I don't want to talk in code around Vickie. Come up with an excuse to get him out of here. "Yeah, Vickie's not feeling well."

"Need to get some medicine? That's too bad. But hey, I actually want to pick up some Red Bulls. I'll tag along."

"Um, that would be fine, Steve, but it's not medicine we're going for." Alexis shot a knowing glance to Vickie. She had a good way of getting rid of Steve.

"Oh. What is it, then? Are you hurt?"

"No, it's…girl stuff. You know."

It took him a moment to process what she was hinting at. "Oh. *Oh!* Oh, okay. Um, tell you what, you two go take care of that. I'll hang back and go later. Maybe somebody else will want to go in a little bit." He ran off quickly.

Vickie laughed but was confused by his reaction. "What just happened?"

"Boys." Alexis shook her head as they began walking again. "If you want to see a boy squirm, start talking about female problems. One mention of the word 'period' and they lose their minds. I knew if he thought that's what this was about, he'd scurry off and we wouldn't have to worry about him following us."

"You sure know a lot about boys, Alexis."

"No, I don't. It just seems like I do. That one is easy. If you ever want to get rid of a boy, just tell him you're having female problems. That'll take care of it. Always does."

They chuckled as they crossed into the parking lot of

the Pick 'n Save. Vickie stopped where she was, right in the middle of the parking lot.

"What's up?" Alexis turned to look at her, then swatted away a mosquito buzzing around her face. "Stupid bug. It's too early for you to be here. Vickie, what's the hold-up? Are you okay?"

Vickie slowly stepped forward to continue heading toward the entrance of the store. "Yeah. I just… Huh. I don't feel so hot, and I don't know why. Whatever the feeling is that's tripping my instincts, it's getting stronger."

Alexis furrowed her brow. "Maybe if we get inside the store, you'll feel safer." Vickie nodded. "Stick with me. Nothing's going to happen to you as long as I'm here, right?"

"I don't…I don't know. I don't really know what this feeling is telling me."

The two girls walked through the automatic doors of the store and were met by a blast of cool air from the coolers holding flowers. Alexis pointed to the racks of bouquets. "I can't tell you how many times I've seen some dude in school walking around carrying one of those cheap things." She shook her head. "It's, like, the lowest form of romance. Everyone does it, they all look the same, and it's like the easiest way to suck up to a girl."

Vickie laughed, but she wasn't listening. The environment of the store was unsettling her.

The vibe of a twenty-four-hour grocery store was always at its lowest in the wee hours of the morning, and that particular Pick 'n Save was no exception. The aisles were empty. The twenty-year-old muzak blaring over the speakers somehow sounded creepy. It felt like a ghost town.

A lone stock boy wandered the aisles, dragging along a rolling cart full of merchandise that needed to go up on the shelves. An unshaven man in a Pick 'n Save shirt rode a floor buffer through the store. The only cashier at the front of the store sat bleary-eyed, leafing through a magazine and hoping the clock would move a little faster.

Vickie and Alexis were not the only customers in the store, however. A few lonely single men pushed their carts through it, stocking up on convenience food, stuffing boxes full of heavily-processed foods between the cases of beer already in their carts.

One woman leaned on her cart as she rolled it around, with her wide-eyed two-year old boy bouncing and laughing.

The sight caused Alexis to squirm. "I hate that," she whispered. "Take your kid home and put him to bed! Geez!"

The girls walked halfway through the store before heading to the back, where coolers full of deli meats and other substantial-yet-affordable goods could be found. "None of this stuff needs to be cooked," Alexis said as they approached the sandwich meat. "You can stock up here and get some good protein. That should settle you down, right?"

Vickie pulled off a package of cooked ham from its hook and stared at it. "I guess so. Maybe grab a loaf of bread or something, and I can build sandwiches."

"That's a good idea. Wash it down with Pepsi. Those are

at the front of the store, though. We can get those at the register. Come on."

They walked down the cereal aisle, admiring the tempting boxes of sugary treats, and again Vickie stopped in the middle of her stride. This time, she clutched her stomach.

"Okay, that's definitely something." Alexis moved in and lowered her voice. "What is it? Can you tell?"

Vickie's wide eyes were fixated on the cracked tile floor. "Whatever it is, it's here."

Alexis' throat closed in panic.

Jim Trembo walked through the front doors, confidently strolling past the flowers and the produce. His stomach was in knots too, but to him, that was a good thing. *Feel that energy coursing through your veins, Jim. Who would've thought you would justify your career—your entire existence—at almost 4:00am on a Friday morning? Next to a high school?*

Even though he was feeling good, he still had to find the girl. Trying to look natural, he grabbed a cart and went to the back, and began pushing it, slowly moving past each aisle and peering down it to see if she was there.

One by one, he moved closer to the cereal aisle.

Meanwhile, Vickie and Alexis were trying to figure out what to do next. "We need to get out of here," Vickie whispered. "I have a feeling that if we stay here, whatever this is will catch up to me and it is all going to be over."

"Over? How?"

Vickie didn't answer, but she shot Alexis a look that told her all she needed to know. Alexis nodded and grabbed her arm. "Fine. Let's ditch the food." She tossed the sandwich meat and the bread onto a shelf next to boxes of Cocoa Puffs.

"Hey, that's not where those go." Vickie stopped to pick them up, but Alexis swatted her away. "That's not right."

"I'm not saying it is, but we're trying to get you out right now. Would you like to get killed or whatever because you felt bad about wasting a package of sandwich meat? Seriously, Vickie. This isn't about being good or proper right now. We're trying to survive. Now follow me, but don't draw any attention to yourself."

Vickie's heartbeat began to race. Her fangs were protruding now, nearly poking out of her mouth. She squeezed her lips together to keep them hidden, and her nose whistled as she panted heavily.

As they reached the front of the cereal aisle, Jim Trembo looked down it. His heart jumped when he saw them. *That's her. Holy cow, that's her. That's the girl. I found her. She's here. I knew it. Now, I just have to go get her.*

He pushed his cart down the cereal aisle, trying to move swiftly enough to catch up with them before they reached the exit.

The girls kept hustling, though. They squeezed past the registers and made a beeline for the exit.

Vickie, however, was shaking her head. "It's not working. We don't have time. Don't look back, but we're not going to get away in time."

"That's ridiculous! Don't talk like that." Alexis pulled on her arm. "Come on. You can still use your speed, right?"

Her mouth hanging open, Vickie disagreed. "No way! How am I supposed to do that in public? I'll get caught again!"

"Not at 4:00am, you won't! Let's just get clear of the doors, and then we can do whatever we have to do in order to get away. Come on."

A wave of excitement rushed through Jim Trembo's body as he reached the front of the store, seeing the girls near the exit. He ditched his cart, sliding his way through the registers as well. Pumping his legs in a power walk, he patted the gun in the holster on his hip, concealed by the dark jacket he was wearing. *Just get them cornered. Nobody's around at 4:00am, anyway. The sun won't be up. This is perfect!*

But the girls reached the fresh air first, and once they did, Alexis stopped Vickie. "Pick me up and let's get out of here. Now."

While she was reluctant, Vickie scooped up Alexis in her arms like a big baby. She didn't need to warm up her powers, simply tapping into her super speed and taking off in a flash…just as Jim Trembo reached the outside.

He blinked, and they were gone.

For a moment, he stood there in shock, then hung his head in frustration. *You should have brought the sword. You didn't, because you thought you could outsmart and overpower a teenage girl. What were you thinking? Sloppy work. Now you missed your chance. She's going back to the school, and she's going to be around people the rest of the night. She knew you were there, and she's going to make sure that she's never alone from now on. You blew it, Jim. Go back to the hotel and get some sleep, because you need a new plan.*

The girls stopped at the entrance to the parking lot. Vickie's stomach pain was dissipating, and she felt relieved. "We did it. We got away from whatever that was. *Whoever* that was. We're in the clear, at least for tonight, I think."

Her stomach rumbled. "But if I wasn't hungry before, I'm hungry now."

Alexis took her hand and led her into the school parking lot. "Come on, maybe somebody has some food that they can share. We'll just say we were at the store, but we didn't have enough money for everything. Then maybe someone will share with us."

The two girls re-entered the party, laughing as they thought about Vickie cradling Alexis like a baby as she ran along the street. The tension had been broken for the both of them, and they were wide awake now.

CHAPTER SIXTEEN

The next morning, on the other side of town, Craig pulled his SUV into a small parking lot in front of a Starbucks coffee shop. Rather than get out of his car immediately, however, he sat in the driver's seat and stared at the front door. As he often did when he was alone, he spoke out loud.

"The Starbucks in Germantown. Well, Craig, you haven't been here since Carol died. This used to be one of your favorite places, and now you're going in there to meet another woman. Don't let yourself get too caught up in that, though. Carol told you she was fine with you dating again. You're not going in there to erase her memory. You're just trying to move on, and there's nothing wrong with that, man. Nothing at all."

He inhaled deeply through his nose and exhaled loudly out of his mouth. Then he cut off the ignition and stepped out of the SUV.

The sun was shining brightly. *I wonder how the girls are*

doing in the parking lot? He looked at his watch. *It's 6:30. They're probably starting to wake up so they can hit the showers and get ready for the day. I bet they're tired as heck.* He smiled to himself as he approached the entrance.

Before he could pull the door open, he saw a couple sitting at a table outside on the patio. They seemed to be deep in conversation. Occasionally, the man would place his open hand on the table, and his partner would place her hand in his.

The sight took Craig back to his days of sitting outside with Carol at a table very similar to that one. They'd laugh at the fact that they were trying to have a nice cup of coffee together while sitting next to the drive-thru exit. Cars would whizz past, spitting exhaust at them. Some drivers had their music blasting. For whatever reason, it never bothered them, just like it didn't seem to bother that couple.

Must be a love thing, I guess. When you're entranced by the person you're with, who cares about the rest of it?

Not wanting to look strange as he stared at them, Craig shook it off and pulled open the door. The strong smell of coffee hit his nose, and he smiled. *Man, you forget how long it's been since you've been in a coffee shop until you walk into one.* He had met dates for coffee in other places, like cafes, and even McDonald's one time, but he hadn't been back to a coffee shop.

This was by design, actually. When Carol worked long hours, she wouldn't be around to spend time with him during the day, and she'd be too tired to talk in the evening. Not wanting to sacrifice their relationship to work, they would arrange to meet at Starbucks in the early morning hours so they could sit with a cup of coffee and enjoy each other's company, free of the responsibilities their careers foisted upon them.

It was one of Craig's favorite traditions, and it had died with Carol's cancer diagnosis.

He wasn't expecting to feel so emotional when he walked into that particular Starbucks, but he was relieved when he saw that his date wasn't there yet. Rather than stick around, he rushed to the back of the store to duck into the bathroom for a moment.

After locking the door behind him, he placed both hands on the sink, looked into the mirror, and began to sob. Tears flowed down his cheeks and he hung his head, watching them drip off his face and into the porcelain basin. He didn't want to get them on his shirt since they wouldn't dry by the time he went back out there.

A few hard sobs later, Craig had composed himself. He looked in the mirror again and saw his bloodshot eyes, heavy with tears.

To his disappointment, the bathroom had *gone green*, so there was only a hand dryer in place of paper towels. *So much for soaking up the tears. I guess you're using your sleeve or the toilet paper.*

Blinking, Craig took some deep breaths and got his emotions under control. He stepped back from the mirror and gave himself a once-over. *Okay, now you just look tired. I think that will work.*

He emerged from the bathroom and saw Katie Adam standing in line for coffee. Before he walked up to greet her, he admired her. *She hasn't aged since high school. My goodness, does she look great! I'm an old, weathered dude, and she's as much of a bombshell as ever.*

Katie was wearing a tight-fitting black blouse with light gray stripes and a black skirt. She looked all-business, with her hair straightened and falling to her shoulders. It looked effortless, although Craig knew better, and it made him feel good that she had gone through the work of looking that good for their little meet-up.

"Katie?"

"Craig!" Her face lit up. "Good morning!" She wrapped her arms around him and embraced him tightly. "I was worried you were going to stand me up."

"Oh, please. Nobody would stand you up."

"Ah, you'd be surprised how often I've been stood up in my life." She laughed it off. "What are you getting?"

"Um, I don't even know." He stuck his hands in his pockets and turned to face the menu. "I just got here. I haven't been to a Starbucks in a long time. I guess I'm just going to have a caramel macchiato. That's what I used to get all the time here."

"You've got a sweet tooth."

"I do!" He laughed. "I like coffee, but I want it to have flavor."

"I'm a black coffee girl myself."

"Black clothes, black coffee. You've got a dark soul, don't you?"

She laughed at his terrible joke. "I've got a few skeletons in my closet, Craig, but I don't reveal those this early." She winked at him, and they both ordered their drinks. Craig stepped forward and paid for both of them, and she thanked him for it.

While they stood at the far end of the counter, waiting for their order, Katie peered at his face. "You look tired. Is this early for you?"

He waved it off. "Ah, I just had a rough night of sleep. The girls spent the night at the high school, doing an all-nighter for the last day of school. I had the house to myself. You'd think I would enjoy that, but I've gotten so used to the two of them being there that I guess it was a little unsettling for me."

Katie nodded. "I know how that is. Well, you could have rescheduled if you were going to be this tired."

"Nonsense! I still have to work today. The world doesn't stop moving just because I didn't sleep well last night."

"Eh, you're right about that. Oh, there are our drinks."

They picked up their coffees and sat down at a table near the window. Craig stood next to his chair, politely waiting for her to sit first.

But she didn't right away. "Oh, hang on! Before we get to talking, I just wanted to see if they had that new dark roast in. Sit down, don't wait for me. I'll be right back." She hustled over to the shelves holding the bags of coffee beans as Craig sat down in his chair and scooted forward.

He rested his elbows on the table, cradling the hot coffee in his hands. Staring across the table at the empty chair, his mind's eye saw Carol sitting there, smiling at him with that gleam in her eye she always had whenever she looked at him. It was the gleam of love and admiration. If there was one thing he missed about her, it was that look. When she looked at him that way, nothing else in the world mattered to him. He knew that the love of his life loved him back, and that kept him going, even in the darkest of times.

Craig thought of the hours of conversations they'd had in coffee shops, planning their wedding, discussing whether they were going to try to have a baby, determining when they would go to their birth class, and so on. He never realized how many major life decisions had been made during their little conversations, the times they'd gotten away from their busy and frantic lives to be together.

Katie returned and plopped down in the chair, sighing openly. "Sorry. They don't have it yet. Maybe it'll be in next month or something. Didn't mean to ditch out for a second, I just always forget to look when I'm here."

"It's no problem, Katie. Don't sweat it."

"Well, how have you been? It's been years!"

"I'm good." He nodded and looked down at his coffee. "I mean, I guess you've been on Facebook, so you know what's going on in my life. The podcast is going very well. My daughter is finishing her sophomore year at Clear Lake. We took in a distant cousin over last summer, and she's also a sophomore at Clear Lake. It's been nice to have another female presence in the house, since..." He didn't finish the sentence, not wanting to bring down the mood.

Katie tilted her head and gave him a half-smile. "Right. I was so sorry to hear about Carol. I know you two loved each other very much. You'd been together for a really long time."

"Oh, I don't need to depress you before you start your day," he said politely.

"Don't talk like that. Carol was a big part of your life! You can't just ignore that. I wouldn't ever expect you to pretend she never happened."

That little comment had an impact on Craig. For so many dates he'd set up on various apps, he'd had to act as though his wife never existed. But here was a beautiful woman who openly talked about her, and wanted him to acknowledge her. She was encouraging him to be himself and deal with his emotions in a healthy manner.

He wasn't used to that. Then again, he didn't know what dating was supposed to be like.

Regardless, the two of them talked for the bulk of the planned hour they spent together. Craig didn't spend the entire time talking about Carol, but when she came up naturally in the conversation, he didn't shy away. For her part, Katie engaged in the conversation as well, even during those parts.

By the time their hour was up, Katie looked at her watch disappointedly. "I really don't want to cut this off, but I have to get to work. What are you up to today?"

"Planning, mainly. I'm brainstorming the next season of the podcast and enjoying the silence around the house during the day. This is the last day of the school year, so after this, they're going to be around all the time. Going to do my best to take advantage of my freedom."

They both stood up and walked to the door, dropping their empty cups in the waste bin. Once they reached the parking lot, Katie turned to face him.

"This was a lot of fun, Craig. I loved getting to talk to

you again. Let's do this again, but maybe at night? Soon, okay? Call me." She leaned in and gave him a warm kiss on the cheek.

Craig paused before heading to his car, opting to watch her walk to hers. He was surprised by how comfortable the morning had been, and he was excited to see where it would go from here.

CHAPTER SEVENTEEN

Jim Trembo rocked as he sat at the table in the small dining area of the hotel. He lifted his wrist to check the time, and his hand trembled. *It's only six. School won't be out for hours.*

A few drops of coffee spilled over the rim of his mug, running down the sides and dripping into his lap as he sipped it. He didn't notice, and his pants were black anyway.

Someone who worked for the hotel shuffled into the room and unlocked the case of muffins and doughnuts, flipped a switch to turn on the orange juice machine, and placed a gallon of milk on the counter. He walked away without saying anything.

Perfect. Maybe breakfast will perk me up.

Jim hadn't slept the rest of the morning after he returned. He'd spent the twenty-minute drive from the supermarket to the hotel planning to grab the sword and head back out again. The thought of finishing the job, knowing the power of the sword and its ability to deactivate Vickie's powers, had excited him so much he couldn't calm down.

It hadn't been until he'd walked into his hotel room that he'd realized she wouldn't be alone for the remainder of the day. School would be in session soon, so he had missed his chance to catch her beforehand.

Because he couldn't come down from his excitement high, he'd walked down to the lobby, poured himself a cup of coffee, and waited for the continental breakfast to open.

As he selected a rock-hard muffin from the plastic shelf and put it onto his tray, a short, bald man walked up next to him and grabbed a tray. He exhaled loudly as if breathing had become a chore in his old age, and he snagged a chocolate chip muffin.

"I like the chocolate ones," he said before releasing a cackle. "What brings you here, my friend?"

Jim delayed his response for a moment, the question barely registering in his brain. "Oh, um, I'm just here for breakfast."

Another cackle. "No, I mean, why are you in Milwaukee? Business or pleasure?"

"Both." *Getting my hands on this vampire and legitimizing my business is a big reason, but man, I will enjoy it.*

"I hear ya. You know, they say if you love what you do, you'll never work a day in your life. I like that."

"Yes, sir. Well, I'll be…"

"We're in town for my granddaughter's wedding."

"Congratulations." Jim didn't hide the bored tone in his voice. He just wanted to be left alone, but this guy wasn't having it.

"Yes, sir. Thank you, thank you. She's getting married

up there in that Florian Park. We wanted to stay down this way because my wife has an old friend who lives in Franklin. Figured we'd split the difference and stay in the middle."

"Very nice. Well, I'm going to…"

"We're from Florida, actually. Yep. Moved down there 'bout eight or nine years ago. A little easier down there in the winter, I'll tell you that! Buddy, you look like you need some sleep. Got bags under your eyes that make you look like you're wearing makeup or somethin'."

Rather than respond, Jim walked away from him as the man shook his head. "Rude. No manners anymore. Nobody wants to talk."

Ignoring the comments, Jim plopped down at the table and sank his teeth into the muffin, which crumbled into dozens of pieces on the first bite. He scowled as he chewed the dry, crusty muffin and choked it down with cheap orange juice. *I might have to go take a nap or something. If I show up at the school and she has no powers, I could lead her away from the school without drawing any attention. I'm a hall monitor, right?*

Back at Clear Lake High School, the day was filled with farewells and cheers. The entire student body was filled with the pre-summer vacation energy that saturates the hall of a school at the end of May.

Vickie approached her locker, which was now a different shade of blue than the rest of the lockers in the area. The new door was almost blindingly bright, reflecting the fluorescent lights into the eyes of anyone who walked past.

A small contingent of students was not quite as bouncy.

The twenty or so who participated in the last night cele-bration looked out of sorts compared to the rest of the student population.

Eric couldn't help but comment on it when he approached Vickie at her locker. "Rough night?"

She smirked. "You could say that. Hang on." Vickie slipped her phone into her hand so she could pull up the email with her new locker combination. "Hopefully, I'll have this memorized by next year."

"Yeah, I saw them replacing it. What happened?"

Vickie quickly glanced down the hall and lowered her voice. "Me."

"You? What did you do?"

"Megan Fitz was getting to me. I was having a bad day, and she just took it too far. I wanted her to shut up, so I punched the locker. Just about caved it in."

Eric shook his head in disbelief. "What happened to you then? Did you get in trouble?"

"No."

"What did you tell them when they saw it?"

"Nothing. I told them I wasn't here and didn't know why it looked that way. Somebody must have hit it with something. I got charged the cost of a locker but nobody knew exactly what happened."

Eric stepped in closer. "Are you…like, is that going to be a thing?"

"What?"

"Sudden acts of violence. I don't want to say the wrong thing to you and wind up getting my face caved in or something stupid like that. Do you have control over it?"

Poor guy. This is still a lot for him to take in. "I have

control over it. That wasn't a sudden outburst for no reason. She poked at me for a little too long. Besides, I took it out on the locker instead of the girl, right?"

Eric nodded. "I suppose so." He rested his head on the lockers forlornly.

Just as Vickie was about to ask him if he was okay, Megan Fitz walked past with her cronies. Vickie braced herself for some kind of vocal attack on her. Instead, Vickie gave her the stink eye, which she'd only just discovered. In response, Megan kept her distance and hurried down the hall.

Vickie smiled and turned to Eric. "You were saying?"

He rolled his eyes and laughed. "I've never seen you make that face before."

"It's a new one for me. Felt a little weird, but it worked."

"I'm going to miss you this summer."

The statement confused Vickie. "What are you talking about? Are we not dating in the summer?"

"No, but I see you every day now. I'm used to it. I like it. But I'm not going to see you every day after today."

She unzipped her backpack and dropped it on the floor in front of her open locker. "I never thought of it like that."

"Right? We get every single day together. I don't want to lose that. I mean, I don't want to stay in school all summer either, but…"

"We'll have dates, and we can hang out whenever you want. I'm only going to be working three shifts a week this summer."

Eric seemed intrigued by the schedule. "You don't have anything else going on. Why would you only work three shifts a week?"

She knelt by the backpack and began shoving loose papers into it. "Hey, I'm plenty busy. Besides, we're doing well financially. My cut of the podcast gave me a lot of money for a teenage girl. My uncle forced Alexis and me to get jobs, so I'm going to do the minimum amount of work required to keep the job and keep him from getting frustrated at me for not working."

He sighed. "I don't know. I just think it's going to be really difficult to see each other. I'm going to miss you. How do I go through my day not getting to greet you in the morning?"

"Well, then, we should just get married."

Eric's jaw dropped. "Excuse me?"

She stood up. "Why not? People do it all the time back where I come from."

"As *teenagers*?"

"Sure. When you're ready, you're ready." She paused, letting the idea seep into Eric's mind. "I'm just kidding." She burst into an uproarious laugh. "You should have seen your face! Really, you were worried that I meant it?"

"Well, no…" His face indicated otherwise. "Look, I have to go clean out my locker before my ride gets here." He kissed her on the cheek. "This weekend?"

"Sure. Come over on Saturday, and we'll hang out. I think Craig's going somewhere, but Alexis and I are both off work."

"Actually, I am hoping we'll go out tonight, too. Let's do both days. Ease me into the dark Vickie-less days of summer."

"Just text me on where you want to go, and we'll make it happen."

He nodded and merged into the hallway traffic to head to his locker.

Cleaning out her locker didn't take Vickie very long. The inside door, which had been plastered with pictures, cards, and notes that had accumulated all year, had been replaced by the new one. All she had to do was stuff papers and notebooks into her bag and close the door.

When she stood up, her stomach twisted. She knew better than to shake it off or ignore it. Instead, she texted Alexis to meet her there because she wasn't feeling well.

Knowing what that meant, Alexis dropped everything and ran to the other side of the school, showing up at Vickie's locker in less than three minutes. "Are you okay? What is it? Is he here?"

Vickie looked at the ceiling, deep in concentration. "He's not here yet, but he's coming. This isn't over."

"What do you want me to do?"

"I don't know yet. Just stick with me for now."

Alexis nodded. "Of course. We're going to be out of here in a few minutes anyway. I'm just about done with emptying my locker. I'll hang with you here, and we'll stop at my locker before we head out. Okay?"

"Okay."

Steve Molenda shuffled past the girls with a smile on his face. "Come on, girls, school's out! What are you still doing here? Wrap it up!"

Alexis used the moment to poke a little fun at a popular kid, even if there were few around to hear it. "We're going, Steve! Keep your pants on for a change!"

He spun and walked backward down the hall, laughing

at the remark. "Nice. Hey, a man's gotta make a few bucks somehow!"

"Whatever. You'd probably make more money getting people to pay you to *not* streak!"

He shook his head, reversed, and continued down the hall, laughing.

Vickie glanced at Alexis. "Aren't *you* comfortable with Mr. Star Athlete."

She shrugged. "How often do you get to make fun of one of the most popular kids in school to his face and not have any consequences? Had to take it."

CHAPTER EIGHTEEN

Vickie's face twisted in discomfort as she lugged her overstuffed backpack down the hall at Alexis' side.

"Are you making that face because of your instincts or because you have too much stuff in your bag?" Alexis joked.

"It's a little of both, honestly. I didn't realize I had so much heavy stuff in my locker."

The two girls reached Alexis' locker, and Vickie groaned after she dropped the bag to the floor. She arched her back, trying to stretch her muscles, keeping one hand on her stomach.

"You look like a wreck." Alexis unlocked the combination lock. "Do you need anything to eat?"

"I don't think so. Not yet, anyway. I bet by the time we are halfway home, I'll be so hungry I'll want to die."

Alexis pulled papers and notebooks out of her locker. "It's funny how much junk you accumulate in your locker in a year of school." One by one, she paused to look at the papers she was holding. "Like, this thing. I wrote it in October. What's it still doing in here?"

"I shoved everything in." Vickie tapped her backpack with her toe. "I'll go through it later and throw stuff out."

"I don't feel like wasting my energy carrying this junk any farther than I have to. Why do you think your bag is so heavy? You saved everything."

Vickie sat on her backpack, using it as a makeshift stool. "I don't even know what I'm supposed to save and what I'm not. This is still new to me, you know?"

"So, how was your first full year of school in twenty-first-century America?"

Vickie thought it over for a second. "Eventful." She laughed. "I feel like so much stuff happened in just, what, nine months? The world is completely different to me now than it was at the start of the school year."

"That's how you know you had a good school year." Alexis nodded confidently, then stood on tiptoe to check the top shelf of her locker. "I'll be honest; I've never had a more eventful school year than this one. Bringing in a new roommate will do that, I imagine."

Vickie laughed, but the pain in her stomach was spiking again.

By the south entrance of the school, Jim Trembo parked his car, stepped out, and walked back to the trunk. Looking both ways before opening it all the way, he reached in and pulled out the long, ornate sword, the one the Circle had used to eliminate the vampire race.

Still in the black clothing from the previous night, he strapped the sword to his waist, letting the blade hang freely. This would allow him to stand sideways and obstruct the view of anyone walking past.

After he strapped it on, he placed his fingertips on the hilt. *You've done so much work for the people, sword. Now is your chance to finish it.*

"Hey, isn't that the hall monitor dude from a couple months ago?"

Two freshmen boys pointed at Jim from far away in the parking lot. He could hear their snickers, knowing full well that they were making fun of him in some fashion. Despite that, he ignored them. Instead, he focused on the south entrance.

Jim knew that was the door Alexis and Vickie left through at the end of school every day. Since school had let out and there weren't many students around, this would be a perfect opportunity to take her.

While he paced at the door, he pulled out his phone and texted Pete Stabone, telling him he was about to get the vampire.

Only a few minutes away from having her in my grasp

Please be smart. She's just a girl

She's not, and you know it. Don't get all soft on me now. This girl will make my career

What if someone is with her?

Probably just the girl she lives with. She has to know she's living with a vampire, right? You can't hide that

You're not going to do anything to her, are you?

She's not the one I want. The vampire is. If she tries to pull something, I can use the sword

Jim...

I'm not going to kill her! Geez. I'm just going to let her know I'm armed, and she shouldn't try anything

Pete didn't respond beyond that, opting to forget the conversation had ever happened. Pete Stabone had been worrying about Jim's obsession with this project. Although he had been encouraging at first, he saw that Jim had allowed this case to consume his life, and he would stop at nothing to take this girl.

Jim, for his part, was nearly giddy with excitement. To him, the plan was foolproof. *Nothing is going to stop me at this point. I've got her exactly where I want her.*

The girls were walking to the south entrance when Vickie's stomach twisted even harder. She fell to her knees in the hallway, clutching her midsection.

"Vickie, hang in there." Alexis dropped down next to her. "Can we get you up?"

"Need…to get…home. Out of this school." She held her breath as the pain shot through her body.

A passing boy saw them on the floor and ran over, sliding down to them. "Hey, are you okay?"

"She's fine. Thanks." Alexis tried to wave him off.

"Are you sure? She seems like she's really in pain. Maybe I can help you…"

Vickie looked up at him. "Girl…problems."

"Oh." The boy nodded politely, then excused himself without saying a word.

Alexis laughed. "See how well that works?"

"Going to use it…more." Vickie willed herself to her

feet. They walked down the long, windowless hallway at the back of the school toward the south doors.

As they passed the small area where the faculty elevator was located, Vickie stumbled into the closed metal doors.

Alexis yanked the backpack off her back and slung one of the straps over her shoulder. "Come on. We have to go. Let's get to safety." She grabbed Vickie's arm and draped it across her shoulder, then helped walk her down the hall.

When they reached the doors where Jim Trembo waited anxiously outside, Vickie stopped. She stood up straight as a board, all her limbs stiff.

Alexis had pushed open the door, but let it close again when she saw her just standing there. "What is it? What's going on?"

Vickie stepped back. "It's nothing."

"What? It's something. Come on, don't play games right now."

"No, I mean, it's *nothing*. I feel nothing."

"Isn't that a good thing? So, you're feeling better then?"

"Not this suddenly." Vickie placed one hand on the bank of lockers next to her, trying to steady herself. "I don't feel anything. My instincts. My senses. Everything is gone. I almost feel lightheaded."

Alexis dropped both bags to the floor and looked deep into Vickie's eyes. "What are you saying?"

"This is the same way I felt when the Circle almost got me. My powers are gone. They turned off my powers. That was how they were going to kill me. This is exactly the same."

Alexis looked at the door, then at Vickie. "What do we do?"

"We need to go out a different way. A more public way. The main entrance or something. I can't go through those doors. There's something—someone—on the other side of those doors. If we walk out there, I'm dead."

"Okay, start walking." Alexis shook her head. "I'll text Dad and tell him to meet us at the main entrance to pick us up. Plenty of people upstairs yet." She carefully peeked out the window of the door and saw Jim Trembo standing there. To her relief, he had been looking across the parking lot and didn't see her face in the window. "There's a guy out there. That must be what you're feeling. Let's go."

As they moved away from the south entrance, Vickie winced in pain. "Yep, it's coming back. Definitely had something to do with that guy."

"We'll go home, and everything will be fine."

"No, it won't." Vickie stopped rushing through the halls.

"What are you doing? Let's go!"

"It's not going to be okay, Alexis. It can't be. Whoever this is knew we were going to be walking out of this place at this moment. He knows who we are. We can't hide from him forever." She dropped her eyes. "Either way, I'm dead. He found me at school, so he can find me at home. I have no chance."

"If you don't stop talking like that, I'm going to slap you in the face and tell you to get it together. I'm not going to let any of this nonsense happen to you, okay? We're going home where it's safe, and we're going to be fine there. If he wants to knock on our door, he's going to have to answer to me, and I won't be polite. I'm getting really tired of you having to deal with this instead of enjoying yourself as a teen like the rest of us."

"I just want this to be over. I don't know how to escape from it anymore."

"Right now, you escape from it by putting one foot in front of the other. We can get out the front door where there are cameras and other students hanging around, and we'll get home. We can regroup there."

Vickie didn't say another word for the rest of the trip to the front door.

By the back door, Jim Trembo waited for another hour, trying to look natural while loitering outside a high school.

After that hour, he realized he had missed them. *Shoot, where did they go? They always come out this way. I was sure this would be the moment.* He gazed at the blue sky. *I guess I'll have to find them at home instead of at school. I wanted to avoid that, but if it's the only way I'm going to get my hands on this girl, that's what I'll do.*

Carefully, Jim slipped off the sword and tucked it back into his trunk. *Not going anywhere without this baby anymore.* He slammed the trunk and drove off, leaving the parking lot and nearly cutting off the car carrying Alexis and Vickie.

Vickie squealed, then tried to look cool and downplay her reaction.

"Stupid drivers," Alexis muttered. Then she looked at Vickie. "Are you okay?"

"No. No, I'm not, and I don't know if I ever will be, Alexis. I really don't know."

CHAPTER NINETEEN

Eric stood under the shadow of a giant polyurethane tyrannosaurus rex that was painted bright orange, with a gaudy green belly. It had bright red teeth sticking out of its mouth.

At least, he *thought* it was a T-rex.

Although the creature loomed large, with a ferocious expression on its face and short, stubby arms, the color scheme and odd design of the head didn't scream T-rex.

Eric had spent his childhood looking at that statue whenever his family drove past the Northtown Mini-Golf course, situated in front of the Northtown Cinema movie theatre. It had always fascinated him, even as he stood underneath it inside the black chain link fence of the park.

"Like, what dinosaur is this supposed to be, really? Who paints a dinosaur all these different colors? Such an odd choice, but for whatever reason, I can't help but be drawn to the stupid thing. What do you think?"

"Uh-huh." Vickie stared between the legs of the tall dinosaur-like creature, trying to line up her shot. She clutched a putter with a purple head, letting it dangle next to her matching purple golf ball. By her calculations, she could get the ball in the cup with one swing from where it was, but the ball would have to take a fortunate bounce.

The date hadn't been going well, but it wasn't for lack of effort on Eric's part. Knowing she had been having a rough time recently, and not understanding what that meant for a vampire, he figured taking her out for a fun date would cheer her up and remove some of the stress from her shoulders.

He came out swinging. He wore a silly tie-dyed shirt he had gotten, although he couldn't remember where. It was rainbow-colored, and he loved it for some unknown reason. It highlighted his goofy side, and he thought it would be just the ticket. Combining that with nervous energy and trying way too hard to make a girl laugh, and Eric really thought he would make a difference.

But the T-rex interaction was typical of this date. Eric was trying to engage, but Vickie was off in her own world, failing to realize what he was trying to do.

That didn't dissuade him, though.

While she lined up her shot and stepped up to the ball, he balanced his legs on either side of the putting green, standing on a pair of rocks and extending his arms like the T-rex above him. He plastered a menacing scowl on his face, trying to mimic the poorly-formed monster above him.

"You know, with this shirt, I think he and I kinda match. *Rrrroooowwwrrrr!*"

But again, Vickie didn't acknowledge what he was doing. She took her shot, and it rolled between Eric's legs, between the giant's legs, bounced off a back wall, and landed in the cup.

Eric clapped his hands and ran in for a high-five. "Nice shot! Tiger Woods couldn't have put that one in there any prettier. Of course, he's not as pretty either." *Play on words. Always a crowd-pleaser.*

Vickie met his high five with a weak effort, barely lifting her arm or smiling.

It wasn't that Vickie didn't want to be there. The discomfort in her body stemming from her instincts going haywire combined with her near-constant preoccupation with whatever threat was causing the problems made it nearly impossible for her to have a good time anywhere.

The two approached the next hole, which required them to hit their golf balls up a green shaped like a dinosaur bone. It was all uphill, and the peak was the tallest point in the entire park, according to the sign next to the hole.

Eric pointed at the sign and laughed. "Look at this thing. *Tallest peak in the park!* Give me a break. This place is the size of a postage stamp. I've been in bathrooms larger than this mini-golf park. Talk about hype!" *Come on, these are good jokes. Give me something here, Vickie!*

As distracted as ever, Vickie just mumbled as she lined up her putt. "Mmmhmm."

Staring down at the ball, Vickie's mind drifted back to the day the Circle had lured her into the field behind her house. She remembered and relived that moment when they had her dead to rights and how helpless she had felt. How powerless.

The thought stressed her. Her powers kicked in, and

she inadvertently socked the golf ball as hard as she could. The ball rocketed off the tee box, up the hill, and soared off the peak and into the air.

Eric held his hand to his forehead to block the sun, following the ball with his eyes as it cleared the six lanes and median of Good Hope Road and bounced into the gas station on the other block.

The two of them stood motionless for a moment in complete silence, processing what had just happened.

As expected, Eric was the one who broke the tension. "I don't think you're getting that one back."

Vickie laughed, red-faced with embarrassment. "I'm sorry."

He walked up and put his hands on her shoulders. "Are you okay?"

"I think I need to sit down."

"Let's grab some ice cream."

The Northtown Mini-Golf course boasted three picnic tables painted blue, yellow, and orange, respectively. A vending machine dispensed drinks and the old man behind the counter scooped chocolate ice cream into waffle cones for the occasional snacker.

Vickie sat at the orange table patiently until Eric returned with a pair of cones for them. She took one and licked a drip on the opposite side before thanking him. "I haven't been much fun today."

Eric agreed with the statement, but he knew better than to say it out loud. "Nahhhhh, don't worry about it. Listen, you're obviously distracted by something. I just thought coming out here and having a little fun would cheer you up."

She looked down at her cone. "It's not that. I'm always happy when I'm with you. You don't have to try so hard. I have just been thinking about something that happened a few months ago."

"Was it a high school thing or a vampire thing?" Eric took a long lick of his cone.

"The second one." She ate a little more of her cone. "You know how I said I felt threatened, and that was what caused me so much pain earlier?"

"Yeah."

"Well, it's not the first time this has happened. There was this group back when I was living in Austria—"

"You mean, four hundred years ago?"

"Yeah. You're just taking all this in stride, aren't you?"

He smiled at her. "Everybody's got something weird about them. Go on."

"Anyway, there was this group called the Circle, and they wanted to kill all vampires. They thought we were biters. They made it their mission to rid the world of all of us. That was why I was put to sleep in the first place. The Circle came for my family. They killed my siblings and my parents, and my parents saved me by hiding me behind the wall."

"That's awful. I knew you woke up in the twenty-first century, but I had no idea that was why."

She nodded. "The Circle came back."

"Where? Here?"

"Yep. They were in Milwaukee. They lured me to the fields behind Alexis' house. There were three of them. They weren't scary guys or anything, but they were convinced that they were going to kill me."

Eric licked a drip of chocolate off his fingers. "Yeah, but these were just dudes, right? You're a vampire. You've got the strength and the speed and the…sharp teeth. I mean, come on. Who did these guys think they were?"

Vickie sighed, reliving the experience in her mind. "It's not that straightforward. They had this huge, sharp, ancient sword. I don't know how they got it or where they got it or whatever, but it was the sword they'd used to kill my family."

"How do you know that?"

"Because this sword deactivates my powers. It neutralizes a vampire and makes them vulnerable to attack. They bring this sword in so a vampire can't retaliate and they cut them down."

"You didn't have powers when they were around?"

"No. They surrounded me, speaking about exterminating the vampire race and all this dramatic stuff. No matter what I did or how hard I fought, I couldn't tap into any of my powers. They were completely blocked."

Eric stared her down, watching her expression closely. "How did that feel?"

It took Vickie a long time to answer that question. She hadn't discussed it openly before, and certainly not outside the house like she was. She didn't know the exact word she wanted to use at first. "Helpless. I felt weak. I couldn't do anything. I couldn't fight. I was not myself. I felt like a shell that was just waiting to be destroyed, and they were ready to do it."

He placed his hand on top of hers. "That sounds like it would have been pretty scary."

"It was terrifying. I thought I was going to die right

there in the field." She then explained how she was saved. "Anyway, that was the scariest moment of my entire life, and I was really worried that I had survived four hundred years, just to die almost immediately after waking up."

"That scares you?"

"Yeah, but not because I'm scared to die. It's because…" Her voice cracked, and it closed off her speech.

Eric tossed his cone into a nearby garbage can and scooted closer to her. "Hey. It's okay."

She took a deep breath and composed herself. "My parents gave up everything to save me. Everything. They sacrificed themselves so I could live. I worry all the time that if I were to make it all this way and then the Circle or whoever else hunts me down *wins*, how disappointed would they be? I don't want their sacrifice to have been in vain. I want to honor them."

"You *are*." Eric dropped his sense of humor. "The fact that you're here, integrating yourself back into society, saving people from tragedy… You're using your powers for good things, and that is something they would absolutely be proud of. Don't sell yourself short just because you might fall victim to an attack. That's not your failure."

She rested her head on his shoulder. "You're too good to me. Thanks. I needed that."

For a second, her concerns dawned on Eric. "Wait, so if you're distracted by that, does that mean that the Circle is coming back? Are they trying to kill you all over again?"

"No. It's something worse than that. I just don't know what or who it is or where it's coming from."

He wrapped his arms around her. "Do me a favor; don't

die on me. You're the first girl to stick around. I'd like to enjoy you a little longer."

She giggled. "I'll do my best, babe. I'm sorry I'm letting this get to me."

He took on a sarcastic tone to lighten the mood. "Oh, goodness, how *dare* you let these people trying to kill you get in the way of our mini-golfing date? Get your priorities straight, Vickie!" He winked, and she laughed.

"What are we going to do about that ball I launched?"

Eric shook his head disappointedly. "I have no idea. I'm tapped out. The only reason we came to this ghetto golf course was because I couldn't afford to take you to a good one."

"Time to get a raise on your allowance."

The two of them chuckled as they cleaned the ice cream off their hands and faces, then returned the golf clubs and ran out of the course before the old man realized one of the balls was missing.

CHAPTER TWENTY

Vickie was lying in a fetal position on the couch, clutching her stomach. On the other side of the room, Alexis sat in her mom's old recliner, watching TV.

"Hey, Lex?" Her father poked his head in, then waved his hand to invite her over to him. He lowered his voice as he spoke to her. "I'm thinking about staying home tonight."

"Why?"

"Do you even have to ask? Look at her. She's miserable. As best I can tell, being a vampire is torture. All those special powers seem to keep her in pain."

Alexis looked sympathetically at Vickie, then back at her father. "She's going to be fine. I think she just needs to get her mind off of it. The boys are coming over anyway. She'll perk up then. We'll watch a movie and relax. We'll show her a good time."

"I don't know how much I'm going to enjoy this date if I know you two are here struggling with this. What if something happens while I'm gone?"

"Nothing will happen, Dad. You've got a great girl on

the hook for a change. Go enjoy the date. We'll call you if anything comes up. Keep your phone on."

"That's true." He looked past his daughter into the living room. "Hey, Vickie?"

"Yeah?"

"You going to be okay?"

"Go on the date. Please. You being here won't make me feel any better. Go have some fun."

He cocked an eyebrow. "Alexis, you better call…"

She put up her hand to stop him. "Dad, I will call. Go, please. Have dinner. Flirt. We'll be here when you get back. I promise."

Craig walked into the kitchen and grabbed his keys off the counter. "And about those boys coming over…"

Alexis put her hands on her hips and rolled her eyes. "Lights will be on the whole time. We'll be in the living room. The curtains will be open. Come on, Dad."

"Good." He walked out the door and headed to the car.

Alexis returned to the living room, thinking about what her dad said about being a vampire. She sat down on the couch next to Vickie, grabbed the remote, and turned off the TV.

"Hey, I was watching that," she muttered.

"Is this what being a vampire is like all the time?"

The question got Vickie's attention. She pulled herself into a seated position on the couch. "Huh?"

"You're just…miserable all the time now. Look at you. You're in pain. You aren't enjoying anything about life, you're just constantly feeling like crap. Is being a vampire a life of feeling like crap?"

"Seems that way right now."

"Did your parents feel like crap all the time? These instincts seem like they exist just to torture you more than anything else."

It was a question that Vickie had pondered before. Whenever she struggled with intense pain, she questioned whether it was good to be a vampire. She *had* come to a conclusion as to why she was feeling this way. "When I was growing up, before my parents locked me behind that wall, I was in a world that had much less technology than there is now. People got around less. There were no planes, no phones, no cars. Some people rode horses, but only if they had someplace to go. The only threats to my livelihood were ones that were immediate—people who existed in or near my hometown."

"It's a lot harder today, isn't it?"

"You bet it is. I can feel when there are forces conspiring against me and my safety. The problem is, *conspiring* can be done with a phone call or a text or an email. And these forces can find me much more quickly in a car than they would on foot, which was how they did it in the past. I'm miserable right now, not because I'm a vampire, but because I'm a vampire in the twenty-first century. Threats can develop much faster, and they pose greater risks than they did in the past."

"I feel like it would be like a hot tub, right? Like, you get used to it after a while?" She smiled.

Vickie didn't smile in response, closing her eyes instead. "No, unfortunately, that's not how it works. It frustrates me that I feel like this. I can't keep it together long because there's someone out there who is ready to make their move. I'm starting to worry more about it because I don't have the sharpest instincts right now."

"What do you mean? Are you feeling less pain?"

"No, but I'm used to it now. It doesn't feel any better, but I know it's there, and I just walk around thinking, *Well, yeah, I'm in pain.* If the pain is trying to tell me something specific, I can't hash that out. There's just so much pain that I can't listen to it very often. That's the downside of all of this."

The doorbell rang.

The girls looked at each other, confused. Alexis looked at the clock. "The boys aren't supposed to be here for another hour."

It rang again.

Alexis got off the couch and peeked through the peephole on the door. She couldn't quite make out the figure, but she recognized the shape of a fully-grown man standing outside. She backed away from the door. "It's a guy!" she shout-whispered. "I don't recognize him. We can't answer the door. Let's get out of the living room while the curtains are still open."

Vickie sat up straight. "My powers are gone again. It's him."

Alexis helped Vickie off the couch and across the living room when the mysterious man pounded on the door with his fist. "Hello?" he shouted.

The girls backed away, reaching the hallway as the man continued to pound on the door loudly.

Outside on the step, Jim Trembo shook his head in frustration. "I don't want to have to break the door open, but I will! Just come here, Victoria. I want to talk to you, that's all."

With no answer, Jim moved to Plan B. On the front step, leaning against the wall, were the sword and a brand new ax. Hoisting it by the handle, Jim reared back to swing at the front door.

The girls shuddered while they waited for something to happen. When the ax struck the door and embedded itself in the wood, they both shrieked.

"Keep it down, girls." Jim called in an annoyed-father voice. "If you had let me in, I wouldn't have to do this!"

Another chop with the ax. Splinters exploded from the door with each chop.

"What do we do?" Vickie grabbed Alexis by the shoulders. "I can't tap into my powers. I can't protect you!"

Remembering something, Alexis snapped her fingers. "Yeah, but I can. Follow me."

As the blows from the ax continued ringing out and it slowly worked its way through the reinforced door, the girls scrambled into Craig's bedroom and pulled out his gun safe, which was locked.

The ax continued, and the pace quickened. *Thwock. Thwock. Thwock.*

"Come on," Alexis grumbled while trying to work the gun safe open. "Open already! Come on!" She dropped the box and opened his tall dresser, sifting through until she found the key to unlock it. "There we go! Come on, come on!"

The unmistakable sound of Jim kicking in the door and stomping in like a deranged maniac from a horror movie froze the girls. Alexis' hands shook so much that she couldn't get the safe open.

Jim's footsteps rumbled down the hallway, and soon he emerged in Craig's bedroom with an expressionless look on his face and a large sword in his hands. He lifted the sword and pointed the tip at Vickie.

The girls shook violently. "Please don't hurt us," Alexis begged, choking back tears. "We don't mean any trouble."

Jim's face remained stony. "Hurt you? I don't want to hurt you. I just want *her*."

"Me?" Vickie placed her hand on her chest. "What do you want from me? Who are you?"

"It doesn't matter who I am, but I have spent years hunting supernatural beings. Now that I have a vampire in my country, I have to act. I am taking you into custody of the United States government."

Alexis shook her head. "You can't do that!"

That comment made Jim crack a smile. "I can't? Please, tell me why not? Is it because that's not how we treat our citizens? Should I look a little deeper into who Victoria Hewitt really is? I'm betting she's here illegally."

"Just…take me. Leave her here." Vickie's voice took on a tone of desperation.

"Don't worry, I don't intend to kill anybody, so don't give me a reason to. You're going to help me."

Slowly, Vickie stood up and walked toward him. Alexis reached for her, but Jim just pointed the tip of the sword at her, causing her to sink back again.

As Vickie stood in front of him, she tried everything she could to conjure up extra powers or energy, but they wouldn't come. She was at his mercy, and she had to hope he wouldn't abuse it.

Jim sized her up. "Look at you. You really do look like a teenager. That is funny. I thought I could take you at the Pick 'n Save, but you gave me the slip. Now it's time for all this to be over. You've had your fun. It's my turn."

"What are you going to do with her?" Alexis sobbed.

"I've got a group of researchers back in Washington, DC. They're all waiting to see this vampire girl. I'm going to make sure they know that she's on the way and that I have her under control."

Just as he finished that sentence, Vickie delivered a powerful blow to his midsection, knocking the wind out of him while he was paying attention to the wrong girl.

His face turned red as he began trying to suck air. When he finished up his coughing fit, he pressed the blade to Vickie's neck.

"No sudden movements. You got that? I'm warning you now. Let's not make this any harder than it needs to be."

Without speaking, Vickie walked with him, but he didn't trust her behind him. When they reached the hall, he wrapped his burly arm around her neck and dragged her out.

Alexis sat frozen and helpless, watching her being literally dragged away.

Vickie's limbs banged against the walls of the house as Jim dragged her down the hall.

"Don't fight it, little girl. There's no point." He shook his head, smiling.

They reached the front door, which had been shattered by the ax. Vickie clutched the man's arm, trying to keep the pressure off her throat as her heels dragged on the ground. When they reached the front step and the fresh air of the outside, he changed positions, putting her in a headlock with her face looking up at him and her body behind him.

"I know this is a little awkward, but I need to see where I'm going, and I don't want you going anywhere." He sneered. "Besides, I need to keep this sword by my side. Well, by *your* side anyway."

As they stumbled down the driveway, Vickie grunted and twisted, but she could not overpower the man without her vampire strength. "Aren't you worried someone is going to see us?"

He sniffed, then looked down the block. "Not really.

This neighborhood isn't known for being populated by a bunch of good neighbors looking out for each other. On this side of town, you have to take care of yourself. Works in my favor. They'll just think you're my daughter or something, and I'm taking you home."

"Where are you taking me?"

"I got a place." He looked down at her with a devilish smile.

Vickie didn't know what he planned to do with her, but she was terrified of what it could be. *I need to leave a trail, something that will lead Alexis or anybody else to me. Think, think, think.*

She remembered Jim mentioning the sword being on his other side. She was in a t-shirt and shorts, so much of her lower legs was exposed. *This is going to hurt, but it could totally work.* With all her remaining strength, Vickie kicked her right leg toward where the sword would be.

As she did so, she threw Jim off-balance, and the two of them twirled around for a moment while he situated himself. "Nice try, but I told you to knock it off," he warned. "You're not getting away. And if you try to get away, I'm going to do more with this sword than just point."

Vickie couldn't see anything behind her, but she felt the blood flowing down her leg. *Got it. I just hope it's enough.* She had managed to cut her skin with the blade and was now spilling blood on the pavement that would lead anyone looking for them in the right direction.

Because it was the evening and he was focused on getting through the neighborhood without being caught, Jim Trembo didn't notice the trail of blood behind them.

They crossed the street to the next block.

"One more block to go, Victoria, then you and I are going to sit down and have a little chat."

"What do you want from me? I'll give you whatever you want, just leave us alone."

"Ehhhh, that's not going to happen. I appreciate the offer, though." He dragged her farther, then stopped to catch his breath. "Oof, I thought you were hard to handle when you had powers, but you are exhausting me right now."

"Good."

He laughed. "I know, I know. I'm a bad guy. But you have no idea what I've gone through to get here. This is the crowning achievement of my life."

"What, kidnapping?"

"Kidnapping is only kidnapping when you're taking a human being. You're not human."

"Are you going to hurt me?"

He shook his head. "Not unless you give me a reason to. Cooperate, and nobody gets hurt."

They crossed the next block and turned up the road, as Jim brought her to the home-base house he had purchased for $2,500. "Home, sweet home!"

Back at the Watson house, a panicked Alexis opened the gun safe and grabbed her father's handgun, tucking it in her shorts. Carrying around a gun intimidated her, but she couldn't spend a whole lot of time reflecting on it.

I need to move quickly. Maybe I can find out where they went.

She darted down the hall, past several picture frames that had been knocked to the floor in the chaos. When she reached the living room, she shook her head in disbelief. *He destroyed our house to get to her.* She stepped over the shattered wood to reach the front step, then paused and looked both ways. *Which way did they go?*

As she thought this over, she looked down and saw the ax resting on the front step. *No sense letting this go to waste.* She grabbed it and rested the head on her shoulder, then charged into the driveway.

When she reached the end of the driveway, she saw the splatter of blood on the sidewalk. She gasped.

He's already cut her. Oh, no. Please don't be gone yet, Vickie. Please don't be gone. Stick around. Alexis followed the blood, staring at a trail of drips leading down the sidewalk.

You moron. All you did was leave a path that will lead me right to you. I'm coming, Vickie!

Two blocks away, Jim dragged Vickie into the dilapidated house and threw her onto the rotted wood floor of the living room.

That was when he saw the wound on her leg. "Geez, what did you do to yourself? I didn't do that."

Vickie looked up at him in silence, holding her leg tightly and getting blood all over her hands.

"You're really messing up my nice wooden floor." He kept the sword in front of his body in case she decided to make a break for it. "Listen, I can't keep you in here. We have to go downstairs."

"I'm not going anywhere." Vickie adopted a brave, defiant tone of voice.

Jim's expression fell, and his eyes grew cold. The look on his face chilled Vickie to the bone. He lifted the sword and placed the tip of it on her neck. "Yes, you are. I can let you walk down the stairs on your own two feet, or I can make you go downstairs. You don't want me to make you. Trust me."

Scowling at him, Vickie pulled herself to her feet and limped across the house, through the filthy kitchen, and to the basement stairway. "Can I turn on a light, at least?"

"Sure."

A lone light bulb illuminated at the bottom of the stairs, shining up the stairway. Vickie limped down one step at a time. *I didn't realize how much this cut on my leg was going to hurt.* Vickie had always healed her wounds quickly using her powers, but as long as that sword was in her presence, she couldn't do that.

Once they reached the bottom of the stairs, Jim pressed the blade to her back and nudged her forward. There was a drainpipe coming down from the ceiling and going into the floor. Vickie stepped up to it, and he handcuffed her to the pipe.

He took a few steps back, nodded, and grabbed a nearby metal folding chair. He unfolded it and sat down across from her. "Now, it's time we had a little chat."

Down the block, Alexis hurried along the trail of blood, periodically looking up to see if anyone was out or could see her. A few teenagers hung out on a street corner. They looked at her, cussed at the sight of a young girl wielding an ax, laughed about it, and turned back around, not interested in getting involved in whatever drama was going on.

I've never wanted to live in a better neighborhood more than I do at this moment.

The ax was getting heavy, and the metal of the gun was digging into the skin behind her back, but Alexis continued to move forward. She refused to pause to catch her breath or to give her arms a break. *I don't know how far they went, but I'll go as long as it takes.*

To her surprise, the blood trail only went two blocks before turning down a street. She followed it until she stood in front of the home-base house. "What on earth is this?" she muttered out loud to nobody.

Not wanting to stumble into a compromising situation, she approached the house slowly, both hands gripping the handle of the ax. The neighborhood was rather dark, so the light shining in the basement window was obvious. She crouched to peer in and saw her friend handcuffed to the drainpipe and the man who took her sitting across from her, talking nonstop, almost without taking a breath. He paused periodically to type something on his phone like he was texting somebody.

I need to get into this house, but how do I do it without getting killed? Any noise I make is going to attract him.

She moved to the front of the house and quietly tried to check the doorknob. It was locked. She squinted at it and noticed it was newer than the rest of the door, or the house for that matter. *He replaced the doorknob so he could lock it. He planned this.*

Moving to the back of the house, she tiptoed up the steps to the back door. The doorknob turned freely, but when she pushed on it, it wouldn't budge. *Must be a deadbolt or something. Darn.*

Alexis moved back into the yard and stared at the house. *Is there a window I can get through? How do I get into this house as quietly as possible? I think I have time to figure it out since he's just sitting there talking.* She moved back to the basement window to peek in.

To her astonishment, he was still talking, and Vickie just sat there on the concrete floor, heartbroken.

If he wanted her dead, he would have killed her by now. He was telling the truth. Whatever it is, he's not here to hurt her, but if he's going to take her somewhere, he's going to do it over my dead body.

CHAPTER TWENTY-TWO

Craig stood in front of the P'zazz restaurant with his hands in his pockets. His knees shook, and he looked down to see how obvious it was. *Maybe I can just tell her I'm cold. Would she buy that? I haven't been this self-conscious in a long time. Am I wearing the right thing? Does it look like I'm trying too hard?*

He pulled his hands out of his pockets to adjust the cuffs of his white button-down shirt, which he had rolled up to his elbows. As he did so, he saw a spot of something crusty on the thigh of his dark blue jeans. *Shoot! You look like a slob.* He tried to rub it off with his thumb, but it was dried on, so he scraped it with his fingernail to loosen it.

Craig glanced around to make sure Katie wasn't walking up to him and wouldn't catch him in the act. He smiled as he thought of one of his favorite bits from Jerry Seinfeld's old stand-up act. *Dry cleaning? What is dry cleaning? You can't clean anything dry. What do they do, tap it, shake it, or blow on it? There's got to be some kind of liquid back there.*

You ever have something on your shirt, and you scrape it off with your fingernail? That is the only kind of dry cleaning.

After the spot was sufficiently loosened and brushed away, he stood up straight, trying to appear put together but also casual. He looked up at the stone lion looming above his head. *Nothing says romance like a big, angry-looking beast ready to feast on you.*

Katie walked across the parking lot, and Craig smiled and waved at her. She looked incredible in her tight blue jeans and short-sleeved white top, which was low-cut but not revealing. Black high heels. The woman was every bit as beautiful as ever.

"You look great." *Don't come on too strong, Craig.*

"Thanks! So do you." She laughed as she approached him. "We're almost twins tonight."

"Oh, yeah, white tops and jeans. I left my heels at home this time, though." He clenched his jaw, worried that the joke was much too lame, but he relaxed when she laughed. It was a better start than he'd expected.

He held the door for her, and they walked in. After giving his name to the hostess, Craig joined Katie on the small bench by the front door. She was looking down with a smile on her face.

"What is it?"

"Just something I remember about you from high school."

Uh-oh. This could be good or bad. Either it's something fun, or it's something that is going to make me feel like a high schooler all over again. But I have to ask. "Is it a good memory?"

"Oh, yeah!" She patted him on the knee, a gesture that

wasn't lost on Craig. "You had a reputation as the guy who always held doors."

"Seriously? That's a reputation?"

"Yeah!" She nodded emphatically. "Most of us girls knew you as the boy who would never enter a classroom before a girl. You always stepped aside and let us through first. You opened doors for everyone with a smile on your face. That was totally you back in those days. And it still is!"

Craig grimaced at the thought. "I was hoping you had remembered something cooler."

"Seriously? Think about it; you had a reputation as a gentleman. Someone with manners. Other boys didn't do that. That's why I remember it. The other boys just charged into rooms. They didn't care who was around them. You were polite. That was why I liked you in the first place."

He shrugged. "I wasn't doing anything special. That was just the right thing to do."

She looked in him the eye. "That's what makes it a good thing. You weren't doing it for attention. You were just doing it. That's how a gentleman operates."

Despite his fears, things were off to a *great* start. Gradually, Craig began to relax, feeling comfortable in his skin. They were called to the host stand, and a server led them into the restaurant. Of course, Craig stepped aside to let Katie go ahead of him.

P'zazz was an ornate place, with two levels of white-tablecloth fine dining. While not everyone there was eating in formalwear, there was definitely an air of effort among those who walked through its doors. If you were eating at

P'zazz, you were expected to show a little respect for the place.

Craig ran his hand along the gold rail as they ascended the staircase to their table, which was situated at the edge of the upper level. The two of them sat down and thanked the server who had seated them.

Katie glanced over the golden rail at the floor below, where a long bar stretched out, and a bartender in a white shirt, black tie, and black vest was polishing glassware, waiting for the next customer to pull up a stool. "This place is really cool. I didn't think many places this nice existed on the north side of Milwaukee anymore." She raised her eyebrows, realizing what she said. "No offense. You don't live far from here, do you?"

Craig laughed and shook his head. "No offense taken. Yes, I live right up the road from here. That's kinda what I like about it, though. It's a nice place, but I don't have to drive all the way downtown to get here."

"Do you eat here a lot?" Katie opened the menu in front of her to look at the wine list.

"No, I don't." Craig flipped to the bar menu. "I don't have much reason to come here. It's a romantic place, not one you bring your daughters, generally."

Katie smiled at the server, who dropped off a basket of warm bread and filled their cups with water. "The atmosphere is cool, and I love the architecture. Like, it strikes this really nice balance between casual and formal, you know?"

He nodded. "Do you like baseball?"

"I *love* baseball," she said emphatically. "I'm a huge

Brewers fan. I'm going to the game on Sunday afternoon, actually, with my sister."

"Have you ever seen the movie *Major League*?"

"It's one of my favorites! Come on, a baseball movie filmed in Milwaukee? It's perfect for me." Then she looked around the restaurant and squinted. "Is that why this place looks familiar?"

Craig smiled confidently. "This is where that scene with Jake at the restaurant was filmed."

"Where he calls her on the phone, and she's just up the stairs? Oh, man! That was totally here!"

He couldn't help but smile at her childlike enthusiasm. "Yep, so you're dining in a little bit of Milwaukee history tonight."

"Wow." She took a sip of her water. The waiter came by and took their drink orders, but she couldn't get over eating in a famous Milwaukee location. "How did I miss that? I love that movie. This is so cool. I feel like you should go downstairs and call me from the bar." She laughed again, and every time she did, Craig felt more of his nervousness melt. "You'd think this place would be packed every night!"

He dropped his smile. "Yeah, I think this restaurant is probably going to close soon. You know, this isn't the best of neighborhoods, and while some areas of Milwaukee are able to overcome that, the northwest side here can't. People forget this place exists because they don't come over this way anymore, and if nobody is driving past, nobody is thinking about it. Plus, *Major League* is like thirty years old by now. It's a classic, but it's not like the next generation is watching it as religiously as we did."

Katie grabbed a piece of bread and spread some butter on it with the knife next to her plate. "That's a real shame. There's no respect for the classics. Besides, that movie's like a time capsule. I love seeing the old shots of County Stadium. They do a good job of hiding it and making it look like it's Cleveland, but whenever I see that scoreboard, I'm immediately taken back to my childhood Brewers games."

Craig laughed as he took a sip of the Scotch on the rocks he'd ordered. "I went every year on my birthday for a long time. I always wanted to sit in Vaughn's Valley and catch a home run, but that never came to be. Oh, well."

"Vaughn's Valley! Oh, that takes me back! Robin Yount. Paul Molitor. Phil Garner. Just… that was the good ol' days."

The two of them continued to swap stories, mainly about their childhood Brewers games. Both of them felt their bond strengthening.

Then Craig's phone rang.

Without looking, he reached into his pocket and hit the button on the side to turn off the ringer. "Sorry about that."

"Are you sure you don't need to answer it?"

"No. I don't answer my phone on dates."

"What if it's an emergency?"

"If it's an emergency, they'll call back. I told the girls to double-call me if they really need me. Anyway, you were saying about that time you tailgated with…" He was interrupted by his phone ringing again. Craig gave a polite chuckle. "Excuse me a second."

"Of course. Answer."

He pulled his phone out of his pocket and saw that it was Alexis. "It's my daughter."

"I hope everything's okay."

Craig answered the phone, turning his body slightly away from the table. "Hey, sweetheart, what's going on?"

"Dad. Vickie is gone."

He flashed a concerned look at Katie, then turned away a little farther. "What do you mean?"

"A man came here and took her."

"I don't understand. How?"

"He broke in through the front door with an ax and dragged her away."

His stomach jumped. "Are you okay? Where are you?"

"I'm fine. He said he didn't want to hurt me. He just wanted her. I'm two blocks away. He has her tied up in the basement of an old house on 53rd Street."

Craig took a deep breath and ran his fingers through his hair. "Where *are* you?"

"I'm at the house. I'm out in front by the sidewalk."

"Are you crazy? Get out of there!"

Katie stopped eating, staring at Craig with concern.

"Dad, I'm fine. I needed to know where she was. I'm armed. I have your gun. I just need help."

"Call the cops! Don't call me!"

"I didn't know what to do! I'm freaking out!"

"Alexis, listen to me. Do *not* go in there. Please. Stay away and be safe. I'm coming immediately, and I'm calling the police. Stay on the line."

"Dad, I have to go. I can't stand out here talking. If he hears me, I'll get caught. Just come here and don't make a fuss." She hung up on him.

He stammered as he looked at Katie with regret in his face. "My girls are in a lot of trouble. I need to go. I'm so sorry."

"Oh, I hope everything is okay! Don't worry about it. I'll take care of it here. Please go take care of them."

Craig leaped to his feet and pulled out his wallet, dropping his credit card on the table. "Use this and get whatever you want, or close up. I'm so sorry about this. I will make it up to you."

She took him by the hand. "Stop worrying about me and go take care of your girls."

He leaned over and kissed her on the cheek. "Bye. I'm sorry."

As he rushed out, Katie shook her head, then folded her hands to say a silent prayer that the girls would be okay. *I don't know what's going on, but it sounds serious. Please don't let anything bad happen to them, or to Craig.*

CHAPTER TWENTY-THREE

E ric rolled to a stop at the intersection just down the block from Vickie's house. He was a mixture of excited and nervous.

A full Saturday night to hang out. She'll be home, so that means she should be a little more comfortable. Hopefully. But Mr. Watson won't be around. Total freedom!

It was his first time driving to a date with his newly-minted license. No longer just driving with his temp, Eric reveled in the independence of being able to get into the car and go. In his mind, it was going to change their dating life for the better, just in time for summer.

He was about to pull the car into the driveway, back out, and park on the street in front of the house when his eyes caught the shattered front door.

"What the heck?" he blurted. "What happened to the door?"

Eric pulled farther into the driveway, parking the car next to the front door. He got out and stared at the door in shock. Shards of wood were scattered everywhere. The door hung open, but most of it had been hacked away. What was left was still on the hinges.

Okay, don't panic. Could have been some kind of accident. The lights are on, so they're probably home. Cautiously, Eric stepped up onto the front step and stuck his head through the gaping hole. "Hello?" No response. "Anybody home? Is everything all right?" *Shoot.*

Before walking in, he scanned the living room and saw a pillow from the couch on the carpet. Past the living room, Eric could see picture frames on the hallway floor. *Don't go in there without a weapon. Whoever did this could still be here.* Thinking quickly, Eric jogged back to his car and popped the trunk. He scrambled through the blankets and other emergency items until he could unlock the flap holding the spare tire in place.

Once it was up, he yanked on the small tire iron clamped to the spare tire. He didn't bother to close the trunk. Instead, he slowly approached the front door. He hesitated before he stepped through the door and pulled out and open his pocketknife. *Use whatever you've got, Eric.*

He took a deep breath and stepped in, tiptoeing as quietly as possible. His hands were already sweating.

The living room was fine, other than the pillow on the floor. Taking a cue from every police movie or TV show he had ever watched, Eric didn't bound into the hall. Instead, he pressed his back against the wall and peered around the corner.

The picture frames on the floor are like a trail of bread-crumbs. Follow it, and you'll reach what you're looking for. Don't make any stupid moves, though.

Once he felt confident that the coast was clear, he

rolled into the hallway, still keeping his body pressed up against the wall. He carefully stepped over the fallen frames. *Don't break them if they're not already broken, and don't make noise unless you have to.*

He held his breath, trying not to make any sudden movements. The tension hung in the air so thick, he almost couldn't breathe if he wanted to. It reminded Eric of the scene in *The Shining* where the groundskeeper walked through the seemingly-empty hotel, only to catch an ax to the chest, courtesy of Jack Torrance.

Let's just hope Jack Nicholson isn't waiting in any of these rooms. Using the same peek-around-the-corner method, he cleared each bedroom, first Vickie's room, then Alexis'. When he reached Craig's room, where the light was still on, he shook his head in disbelief.

This place is a mess! I'm guessing they didn't go quietly. He bent over to inspect the thick black box lying open in the middle of the room. *Bullets. This is a gun safe, and the gun is gone...*

"Hello?" a voice called from the front of the house.

Eric gasped and gripped his weapons tighter. He peeked down the hallway to see Charlie standing at the other end, confused.

"Oh, Charlie. It's you." Eric relaxed his shoulders.

"What the heck happened here?" He extended his palms in confusion. "Where is everybody? What happened to the front door?"

Eric charged to the end of the hall and passed him, turning into the kitchen with a determined but worried look on his face. "I don't know. I really don't." He walked to the top of the basement stairs and looked down, seeing nothing but darkness. "I don't think they're down there, either."

"Should we call the cops?" Charlie stepped into the kitchen, still confused.

Eric didn't answer, charging instead out the side door to the backyard.

Still in the house, Charlie threw his hands in the air. "Seriously? You gonna talk or what?" He unlocked the sliding glass door to the patio and walked out to see Eric marching around the pool and behind the shed. *What is he doing?* Charlie jogged past the pool after Eric, finding him standing behind the shed, staring blankly at the field that stretched in front of them. "Why are we out here?"

"I didn't know if the girls were there or not."

"What, hiding in the field? Why would they be out there?"

"Just..." Eric couldn't think of a way to explain what was on his mind, so he just headed back to the house.

"Dude!" Charlie ran after him. "Are you going to talk? Did you do any of this?"

"Really?" Eric looked at him with disbelief. "You're worried that I did this?"

"You seem to know more about what's going on than I do!"

Eric's anger was starting to bubble over. "I don't know *anything*! I know as much as you do right now!" This wasn't entirely true. In fact, Eric was very worried that whatever had happened was related to Vickie's fears. He took his eyes off Charlie and stared at the house from the backyard, trying his best to think of what could have happened. He avoided the worst-case scenarios playing out in his mind.

Charlie watched his eyes moving back and forth. "What are you thinking?"

"I'm just..." Eric sighed, feeling handcuffed by his inability to talk about Vickie's true nature and her grave concerns. "I don't know."

Charlie, shaking his head, pulled out his phone.

"What are you doing?" Eric shot him a glance.

"Calling the cops."

Eric swatted the phone out of his hands, sending it flopping onto the grass. "No!"

"Dude! What are you doing? Obviously, we need to call the cops!"

Eric knew that if the cops were called, they would run the risk of exposing Vickie. He didn't know how to handle this, but he was sure calling the cops was the wrong choice. "You can't. Not until we know more."

"What are you, Batman? We're not detectives here. This is real life! Obviously, the girls are hurt or gone. What are you hiding? You know something."

"I don't know anything. How many times do I have to tell you that?" Eric walked to the driveway.

"You're full of crap. You know something, and that's why you don't want to call the cops. What are the girls involved in? Is there something bad I don't know about?"

"Charlie, now is not the time to argue about this. Holy cow..." Eric stopped in his tracks at the foot of the drive-way, seeing the blood on the concrete. "They *are* hurt."

"Geez." Charlie shook his head. "I'm getting my phone."

"No!"

Charlie gestured wildly at the bloodstain. "What else do you need to know? Do you need any more signs that something is terribly wrong? We're not qualified to handle this! That's what the police are for!" He turned to walk to the backyard.

Eric grabbed him by the elbow and yanked on it. "The police aren't qualified to handle this. Trust me."

Charlie pointed at him with an accusatory tone. "See? You know something. Tell me right now. Tell me right now, or I'm going to call the cops."

Eric stared him down. *He's not bluffing. Come up with something. Tell him enough without spilling the beans completely.* "I can't tell you why. Or, I don't know why, really. But in the past few weeks, Vickie has been very worried that somebody was coming for her."

"Who?"

"I don't know. She didn't know either. Somebody from her past."

"From Austria?"

There you go. That'll buy me time. "Yeah. From Austria. Somebody who knew she was here and wanted bad things to happen to her. She has been very preoccupied with that."

"And you think that's what this is about?"

Eric looked at the bloodstain. "That's my only guess, but I know you can't call the cops."

Charlie rubbed the back of his neck, one hand on his hip. "So, what are we supposed to do? Just sit here and wait for them to come back?"

Eric shook his head. "They might not come back."

"Should we follow the blood?"

"I *want* to, but I don't know who is at the end of this trail. We just have a pocket knife and a tire iron. That might not be enough to fend off these people."

"Then what do we do, Eric? We can't just sit here and putz around if they're in trouble!"

Eric didn't know how to answer that, and in his mind, he was terrified that they were too late.

Back on 53rd Street, Alexis crawled over to the basement window to watch Vickie and Jim again.

Neither had moved. *That's a relief. As long as he's sitting there, he's not hurting her.* She couldn't hear what Jim was saying, but he appeared to be rambling about something, and he kept the sword at his side.

To her heartbreak, Alexis watched Vickie stare at the basement floor. *She looks so defeated. The strongest person I know, and he has broken her. I wish I could do something.* She squinted, trying to get a better look at her friend. *The blood came from her leg, it looks like. Other than that, there's not a scratch on her. He's not doing anything to her. He's not beating her, or worse. He's just talking to her. Did he really drag her all this way and destroy our house just so he could talk to her? That doesn't make any sense!*

Alexis gripped the ax in her hand. The gun tucked into her waistband was calling to her. All she wanted to do was shoot this strange man and save her friend.

If I could just open this window, I'd have a straight shot, but he's sitting really close to her. If my aim is off, I risk hitting her. And if I made any noise opening this window, he could shoot me, too, before I even got set up. Or he could kill Vickie. I can't do that to her. I need to sneak up on him, which means I need to get into the house somehow.

CHAPTER TWENTY-FOUR

As all this was going on, there was very little movement inside the house.

Vickie just sat, dejected and defeated, handcuffed to the drain pipe. Seated across from her in the folding chair, Jim Trembo fumbled with his phone, one hand resting on the handle of the sword at his side.

"Come onnnnn…" he muttered. Then he looked at his captive. "I'm just waiting for a call back from my boss. One of my bosses, anyway. My *real* boss is the President, but he's hard to get on the line. I sent him a picture of you so he knows I have you under control."

Vickie dabbed at her leg wound, which was still dripping blood slowly onto the concrete. It was pooling underneath her. Her body was clotting it, but it hadn't finished sealing the wound yet. She winced as the ache crept up her leg. "And your boss knows you've injured me? I can't imagine any government approving of that."

Jim laughed, scoffing at the notion. "Such an innocent girl in some ways. In desperate times, most of us operate by any means necessary. Besides, you did that to yourself. I didn't poke you with the sword. That was all you."

She sneered at him. "Capturing a teenage girl. An *injured* teenage girl, locking her to a pipe, and taunting her from just out of reach. Do you feel like a big shot, Mr. Grown Man? That you overpowered a high school student?"

"I'm getting jittery." He reached into his pocket and pulled out a pack of cigarettes and a lighter. Sticking one in his mouth, he flicked the lighter a couple of times until a flame popped up. He puffed on the cigarette until the end glowed, then stuck the lighter back into his pocket, along with the pack of smokes. After taking a long drag, he leaned back and released the smoke into the air. "I don't like to smoke often, but I haven't slept in days."

"I know the feeling."

"Want one?" He smirked. "Nah, you're *too young*." He laughed at his poor joke. "Look, girl, you can paint yourself as some weak, helpless victim, but you're no teenager. You're hundreds of years old, and you're a vampire. That levels the playing field considerably. Honestly, for how much I know about vampires and their powers, the field is tilted in your favor quite a bit. It's something of an accomplishment that I've been able to get you down here and under control, so save me the sob story about how unfair everything is. You're vastly stronger than me in a lot of ways. I just managed to neutralize you." He stuck the cigarette back in his mouth.

Vickie shook her head, looking at the sword with disdain. "How did you get that thing, anyway?"

Jim took another puff, then pulled the cigarette out of

his mouth. "The sword? I got it from your friends at the Circle."

"Those aren't my friends."

"Oh, I know." He wore a self-satisfied grin. "They told me a heck of a lot about you and your kind."

"Such as?"

"Well, that you're vampires. Bloodthirsty, evil creatures that suck blood and consume the flesh of innocent people. The guys I talked to called your race a cancer on the world. You survive by victimizing other people. I'm doing the world a service by capturing you before you can hurt anyone else."

Vickie rubbed the cold metal of the handcuff that was digging into her wrist. *Look at how thin this chain linking me to the pipe is. If I had my powers, I could snap these stupid things and get out of here in a flash.* "What are you going to do to me? Why do you want me? You're not here to save the world."

Jim puffed on his cigarette. "Well, we're talking about a science experiment here, among other things. We have never been able to study another race before, at least not in recorded human history. We want you under control for the same reason we tag deer and dolphins in the wild—to learn. This world has vampires, apparently. We're curious."

She shook her head. "So, why don't you just tag me and let me go? You do those things to animals, and you let them go free."

He chuckled with the cigarette hanging off his lip. He glanced down at his phone, then leaned forward in the chair, resting his elbows on his knees. "Okay, bad example. This is more like…penning up horses and dogs. It's not just about learning what you can do. It's also about putting your strengths to productive use."

"What?"

"Horses are strong and have great endurance, more than a human. We put that to good use by learning to ride and control them. Dogs are excellent sniffers. Their noses outperform a man's, so we train them to inspect for stuff like drugs. They are tools we use. It doesn't mean we treat them poorly. Far from it. But we do make them usable so they can be productive members of our joint society."

The comparison left Vickie feeling insulted. "You're talking about animals. I'm a person, not a dog or a horse."

"Pfff. No, you're not." He shook his head and leaned back in his chair. "You're not a human being. You're a vampire. You *look* like a human being, but that doesn't make you one. From a biological standpoint, we're very different. Yes, we have similarities, but we're different. Monkeys look like us, but they're not human. We don't let them into our schools, for example. Besides, you should want to be studied."

"Excuse me?"

"You care about education, right? If you want to help the human race, you should submit to this. Let yourself become a subject of science. Shoot, as a culture, we barely know how the human body works. Every other year, there's another health recommendation, and everyone argues about it. That's just with humans. Now, throw a vampire into the equation, and we're opening the door to an entirely new species! We have to do this in a controlled manner, though. We can't have you running free in our society. You're too much of a threat."

Vickie got onto her knees, trying to take a relaxed posture to counter the relaxed confidence of her captor. "Excuse me? I have full control over my powers, and I pose no threat to anyone. All I want to do is live a normal life!"

"I'd believe you. I really would. But we both know that's a lie." He got up and began to pace, occasionally looking down at his phone. "Victoria, we know you have destroyed property. You've injured people. You've caused accidents. Major ones, too. We have it on video. You demolished a car, injuring an innocent bystander, then ran off, refusing to take responsibility for your actions. Does that sound like a safe, normal member of society?" She didn't answer. "When somebody gets behind the wheel of a car and crashes it, he's not allowed to leave the scene of the incident. If he does, we consider that a crime. People go to jail for that. You caused serious injury, and we even have video of you running away from the scene. You're dangerous and irresponsible. Ironically, you *act* like a teenage girl, even if you're four hundred years old."

Vickie hung her head. She didn't want him to be right, but there was something to what he was saying.

"Now, Victoria, you have strengths. We just need to rein them in and put them to good use. If we know that somebody is an excellent shot with a gun, we want to get them into the military. Give him a sniper rifle and have him take down enemies from long distances. If a person has an aptitude for planning and strategy, we like to get him in charge of a military unit, planning missions and leading people into battle. And I'm talking about *people* here, not animals, so don't give me that excuse. We take men and women with their strengths and find strategic ways to employ them. You're dangerous, Victoria. But you have strengths. We want to harness those strengths and use them. You'll save lives instead of endangering them."

She scowled at him. "But I don't want to. All those people you talked about do so voluntarily. You can't force them to do it. You can't force me to do it either."

He finished his cigarette and dropped it on the concrete floor of the basement, then stepped on it to extinguish it. "You just don't know it yet." He exhaled the rest of the smoke, and a haze hung in the air. "How many dogs do you think want to be drug sniffers? They don't know it, but they have the time of their lives when they get trained for it. It's just a matter of trying it, and they learn to love it. You'll learn to love it, too. Trust me."

Vickie clenched her teeth. "What happens when I get away? I can outrun you and anything you have. I can find a way to hide."

Jim smiled again, meeting her gaze. "Not as long as this thing is nearby." He pointed the tip of the sword at her threateningly. "If I have this near you, you're not going anywhere. You don't have the strength."

"I'll find a way. I have to. You can't keep me penned up forever."

"Ha!" He lowered the sword. "You think you want it that badly? Listen to me. I've spent decades of my life —*decades*—looking for something like you. I've bet my entire career—my life's purpose and meaning—on bringing you into the fold. This moment is everything I've worked toward. You have no idea how focused I am on this. Let me clue you in to something that you don't know because despite everything you say, you are *not* human.

There is nothing stronger than the human spirit. When a man puts his mind to it, he can do anything. He is stronger than anything around him, even a vampire like you." He stepped forward, almost nose to nose with her. "If you escape, I'll hunt you down again. I have nothing to lose anymore. It's all on the line here. My entire existence only has meaning if I keep you under our control."

He straightened and stepped back, glancing again at his phone. "You can threaten me. You can say what you want. You can insist on how awful I'm being to you, or whatever. Truth is, I'm just doing my job, and I will not give up on it. Even if it takes me another twenty years to find you, I'll do it. You can't hide your nature, Victoria. You'll slip up. You'll instinctively lash out at something and show your hand, and I won't be far away." He sat back down in his chair. "In other words, you might as well just give up now, because the fight is over. I've won."

CHAPTER TWENTY-FIVE

Jim's phone beeped. "Finally!" He swiped up on the screen and began texting with one of his bosses. He thought out loud as he did it. "Going to call this guy in just a minute. Get this show on the road! I'd rather have you safely under the purview of the US government than handcuffed to a pipe in the ghetto. I think you're going to like it, actually. We'll treat you well. Better than *this*. You'll probably thank me later."

Vickie didn't hear a word he said. She had tuned out everything around her; her entire being was overcome with grief. That feeling of helplessness she'd described to Eric had consumed her. *I'm a vampire. But without her powers, what is a vampire anyway? Not one. If I'm not a vampire anymore, and I'm not human, what am I? I feel so useless. My existence is pointless.*

"Mr. Casey!" Jim practically shouted into his phone. "What a pleasure to hear from you, sir!"

On the other end of the line, Doug Casey, the head of Homeland Security, sat at a large mahogany desk in his study, surrounded by various books on American and world history. "Jim, why are we all getting these messages from you? What do you have for us?"

"Sorry, sir, I didn't want to simply send it in a text. I've got a vampire."

There was a pause. "A vampire. A real one?"

"Yes, sir! I have her in my custody right now."

Casey tapped his fingers on his desk as he stared across the room at a musket hanging on the wall. "Jim, you know you have a reputation among many departments here in Washington…"

"I understand that, sir." Jim interrupted, not wanting to let the conversation get off-track. "I just need a flight for me and my companion here."

Casey shrugged his shoulders. "Okay, so fly her back. We'll reimburse you."

"No, I need a *military* plane." Jim's eyes widened. This was the conversation he had been waiting so long to have, and now he was getting to make the demands.

Or so he thought. "Just book a flight and use your credentials. We'll cover the bill. Bring her here, and we'll take a look at her."

"You don't get it, sir. I can't fly her without a sword by my side, and I can't get on a commercial airplane carrying on a sword, no matter who I am. This is why I need you guys to send an official flight this way. I can get her to an airport, but I need your coverage to get her out of Milwaukee."

Casey shook his head. "The President has been tightening budgets left and right."

"You don't understand, Doug! This is the biggest development in scientific and military history!"

His boss sighed, pinching the bridge of his nose and closing his eyes. "Jim, you said that about the zombie army experiment, remember?"

Frustration was building in Jim Trembo's body. He paced anxiously. "This is different. I have everything here. I've seen it. This is it. She is going to be the key to unlocking an entirely new and hundred-percent more effective war strategy. She's a specimen, unlike anything I've ever seen."

"So, you've seen her powers in action?"

"Yes! I saw the video!"

Casey shook his head. "No, Jim, I mean in *person*. You saw the zombie stuff on video, too. Videos can be doctored. I can't send an escort on the basis of a video again. That's not proof."

Jim was ready to pull his hair out. "Look, Doug, I've talked to people in the department. You guys gave me the funding to do this. Were you just setting me up as a sick joke? I've gotten us to the finish line, but I need your help to get me across it."

Doug paused. "I can't get you a military plane, Jim. If you can somehow get her here, we'll take a look at her. We'll cover expenses within reason. We're interested in what you're talking about, but only if it turns out to be legitimate."

Jim pursed his lips. "Why are you guys turning your backs on me now? Right when we're on the cusp of a discovery that will change the course of history..."

"I'm sorry you feel we're turning our backs on you. We

just want to make sure there's accountability built into this process. The last time we went through this with you—heck, *every* time we've gone through this with you—you've gotten your paycheck and used up our resources, and we've reached dead-ends. Our government has lost hundreds of thousands of dollars on you. This time, we want your skin in the game, too."

"I can't believe you're hampering this, Doug. Seriously."

"Jim, we want to see her. If you can get her here, we'll take a look. Right now, we can't risk anything more than that. All the best."

After Doug hung up, Jim clutched his phone so tightly, he almost cracked the screen.

Vickie would have savored the moment, but she had withdrawn into her mind, sitting silently with her eyes closed. To her surprise, she felt her blood flowing a little faster, and she was taken back into her memories from four hundred years ago.

How is this happening? I don't have my powers! How could I leap back? Without knowing how to answer that question and with nobody to talk to, she simply savored standing in the foyer of her castle one more time. A lump formed in her throat as she remembered what it was like to be a vampire, free to use her powers within reason, and *able* to use them.

This was when I was myself. This was when I was a vampire. I miss that so much. Nothing good has come from me waking up. I should have stayed in that box or stayed awake and died with my family. That would have been much more honorable than where I am now.

Suddenly, the front door flew open, and her father was

dragging young Victoria into the house, slamming the door shut behind them. Vickie followed the two shadows of the past through the library and into the kitchen, where they sat with her mother, who was slowly cooking meat over the fire.

"What happened, my dear?" her mother asked as she poked the sizzling meat.

"Our daughter was engaging in a conflict with a Sang." He gave her a stern look.

I remember this. It was a boy, and we were really laying into each other. He wanted to bite me, but I fended him off. We were in a field way out of town. Nobody saw us, but my father discovered us as it was happening and dragged me away. I was so mad at him that day. Still, Vickie smiled as she watched the old memory unfold.

"I don't get it, *Vater.*" Victoria slammed her palms on the table. "I was just defending myself!"

"You're right, my daughter, you *don't* get it." He leaned close and looked her in the eyes. "We have taught you that when you are in those situations, you need to remove yourself completely."

"But why? *Mutter*, we are vampires!"

"Yes, lovely one, we are." Her mother gave her a disapproving look. "But we are not to use our powers frivolously. They are for avoiding conflict, not engaging in it."

Victoria crossed her arms, scoffing at the notion. "Then why have powers? That's what makes me a vampire! You should encourage me to be myself. I honor my family line by using the powers that were bestowed on me by my ancestors!"

Her father looked on her almost with pity. "My dear, that is not how you honor your family."

"So, I am supposed to pretend that I am not who I am? How does that show respect to my bloodline?"

He cradled her hand in his. "Victoria, you are a vampire because of your bloodline. *That* is what makes you who you are. Your powers are just powers. At some point in your life, they will fail, but that does not make you any less of a vampire. Choosing to not use them irresponsibly is a wise way of managing your powers, but they don't make you who you are."

He let go of her hand, stood up, and walked over to his wife, wrapping his arms around her. Without smiling, she reached up with both hands and held onto his arms, leaning back into his embrace. "This right here, Victoria. *This* makes you a vampire. The bond we have as a family is what matters the most. It's not about engaging in conflicts. It's not about being faster or stronger. Your family makes you who you are. That family bond is stronger than any power you have in your body. Your body will fail, but the bond with your family never will."

Standing in the doorway, Vickie watched all this unfold with her bottom lip quivering. She held back to avoid sobbing openly. Tears streamed down her cheeks. *I miss them so much. I miss this world. I miss feeling like a vampire.*

Vickie opened her eyes, and she was back in the basement again, still handcuffed to the pipe. Her cheeks were wet with tears, but Jim didn't notice them. He was too busy sending frantic texts to anybody in Washington, hoping someone would listen to him.

The vampire girl leaned her head on the pipe. *You are*

still a vampire, Vickie. That doesn't change just because you can't use your powers. Never forget that.

Although she could not explain how she had been able to access that particular memory, it soothed her, even though she felt helpless.

Also feeling helpless was Alexis, who was still crouched outside the basement window watching her. *That face. She was in her memory bank. There's still vampire left in her somewhere.* The sight of Vickie holding back sobs while stuck in that basement was enough to break Alexis' heart. *I have to get in there and get her out. I won't be able to live with myself if I don't try.*

CHAPTER TWENTY-SIX

Alexis carefully walked around the back of the house to a row of windows. Peeking in, she saw the mess of a kitchen.

Okay, if I can get in here, I'm right by the basement. Nothing in the kitchen to trip over, except for what looks like a bunch of wood in the middle. She set the ax down and leaned it against the house.

There were three windows in the kitchen. Propping herself up on a line of rocks that jutted from the brick exterior, Alexis gripped the bottom of the first window and tried to yank it up, but it wouldn't budge. *Must be locked.* She scooted over to the middle window. A busted screen covered it, preventing her from reaching the frame. *I have to get this out of the way quietly if I'm going to try the window.*

Meanwhile, down in the basement, Jim Trembo was dialing again. Vickie watched him defiantly, mustering just enough confidence within her to make the experience as unpleasant as she could. "Who are you calling now?"

He stopped scrolling and looked at her in surprise. "What do you care?"

"Hey, don't be crabby with me. It's not my fault you're having trouble. I'm just sitting here, exactly where you want me, right?"

Jim sneered at her. "I'm calling a colleague of mine, okay? I'll get you to Washington if I have to drag you there on foot." He tapped on his screen and lifted it to his ear. "Pete?"

"Jim, it's like…10:30 here. What are you doing?" Pete cleared his throat, trying to wake himself up without disturbing his family.

"Pete, I've got her. She's right here. I have to get her to Washington."

"That's great, Jim."

"Problem is, nobody is ponying up. I need a military plane or escort to get her there, but it's not happening." He explained to Pete his conversation with Doug Casey.

"Jim, just out of curiosity, you said you *have her*. What do you mean by that?"

"I mean, she's here." Jim shrugged.

"Where's *here*?"

"I found her and brought her to the empty house I bought. She's handcuffed to a pipe in the basement. I used the sword we found to get her here, since it deactivates her powers."

Back in Virginia, Pete Stabone put his head down on the kitchen counter. "You *kidnapped* her?"

"Knock it off, Pete. We both knew she wasn't going to come easy. A little force was necessary."

"Did you hurt her?"

"No! I haven't harmed a hair on her head. She's got a cut on her leg, but she did that to herself while I was dragging her down the street."

"Jim, I'm just going to repeat what you said to me. You dragged a teenage girl against her will down the street and into a strange, empty house, where you have her handcuffed to a pipe in the basement. She's injured because you were carrying a weapon with you. This doesn't make you sound great."

Jim's rage was beginning to boil over. "Pete, knock it off! I have done *everything* to bring this project to the finish line. I have devoted every last bit of my time and energy to make this happen. Nobody else has dedicated themselves to this like I have. You all wanted proof. I have proof right here, right now. I just need to get that proof to Washington, and the whole game changes. Now you're worried about how it *looks*? Give me a break!"

Pete winced at the thought of what Jim was doing. "Right, but you don't have government backup at the moment. They're not going to vouch for you. If it looks bad, they have all the freedom in the world to distance themselves from you if, say, the cops show up. All the cops will see is that you went crazy and kidnapped a teenage girl to do God knows what. This is bad, Jim. There had to be another way to go about this."

"I didn't call you for a lecture, Pete. I want help getting this girl to Washington."

Pete sighed. "If you can do it without looking like a psycho, I guess you could drive her."

Jim nodded. "Yeah, that's not bad. How long of a drive is it from Milwaukee to DC.? Do you know?"

"Fourteen hours or so, if you drive straight through."

In his mind, Jim weighed the possibility. "I'd have to keep a tight rein on her. She'd have to be, I don't know, tied up or something."

"And when you stop for gas, people will see a teenage girl tied up in your back seat. That looks really good, Jim."

"Okay, if I put her in the trunk…"

"Are you listening to yourself, Jim?"

Outside the house, Alexis carefully removed the screen from the window. It bent easily, and she took it off without making much noise. She tossed the screen onto the grass. *Come on, window, open for me. Please.*

To her surprise and delight, the window eased open, but it was old and tight, and it squeaked with every movement. *Take your time.* She nudged up the window bit by bit, flinching every time it squeaked. She held her breath. *Please don't hear. Please don't hear. Please don't hear.*

Soon, she had the window open several inches. *Not enough to climb through, but we're on the right track. Come on, stick with it.* She slipped her hand in, which gave her more leverage to push up the window.

Jim Trembo didn't hear any of it since he was busy arguing with his colleague. "This is a nightmare, Pete! Everyone has my back and supports me, telling me this is going to work, and I'm going to change the world. But now that I need some help and funding, because *everything is working out the way I said it would*, I'm left high and dry. It's stupid!"

"You have a reputation, Jim. We thought you would have this taken care of by now. That much, I know. Because it's taken so long, there are serious doubts that you know what you're doing. I've talked with Doug Casey and others. The thought is that you're losing it."

Jim kicked the drywall at the bottom of the stairs as hard as he could, sending dust into the air as he knocked a hole in it. "I *am* losing it now! I had it together before, but now that I'm being abandoned, I'm definitely losing it! How can I do my job when I'm handcuffed like this?"

Vickie smirked. "Oh, the irony."

"You shut up!" He pointed at her.

"Don't threaten her, Jim! This was supposed to be a peaceful thing, and you resorted to violence."

"Not yet, I haven't!"

The sound of Jim kicking the drywall stunned Alexis for a moment. She leaned forward, putting her ear close to the open window and hoping she wouldn't hear Vickie scream. To her relief, she didn't. *I hope she's okay. Just a few more inches, and I'm in.*

Back at the Watson house, the two boys argued in the driveway as Craig pulled in, tires squealing. He parked the SUV haphazardly in front of the driveway and jumped out.

"Boys! Are they both gone?"

"Yes, sir," Eric answered. "I didn't know what to do."

"What did the man look like?"

"We don't know. We weren't here," Charlie said. "We got here after the fact. We don't know where they are or what's happening."

"I know what's happening. Alexis called me. They're two blocks away." Craig pulled out his phone. "I have to call the cops."

"Are you sure?" Eric asked. "I didn't because…"

Craig held up his hand. "I know why you didn't. It's

okay. But my little girl is in danger. I don't care what this risks. I need help, and after I call them, I'm grabbing my gun and going after them myself."

"Your gun is gone, sir." Eric raised his eyebrows. "The safe is open, and the gun is gone."

Craig sighed. "Crap."

Alexis had the window open enough. Contorting her body as best as she could, she was able to ease her legs through and just get her toes on the floor. This gave her enough leverage to ease her body through the frame and into the kitchen. *Shoot! I didn't grab the ax!*

Down in the basement, Jim had had enough. "I'm done, Pete. I'm done. I will take this girl to Washington myself, and screw the rest of you. I don't care what I have to do. I'll throw her in the trunk bound and gagged if I have to."

"Don't do that, Jim. You're going to regret it."

"So will all of you. You guys are the reason this is happening. I'm not doing it because I want to, I'm doing it because I have to. If that's what it's going to take, then that's what I'm going to do. I will not give up and let her go. This is everything to me, and I won't stop until the President himself sees her. I'll get a freaking Medal of Honor for it!"

He ended the call and threw the phone across the room. It crashed into the concrete wall and shattered.

"Aren't you going to need that?" Vickie taunted him.

Jim spun and punched a hole into the drywall with his bare hand. Blood dripped down his knuckles. "You heard me. I'm getting the car and throwing you in. If you make a noise, I'll gag you. I don't want to, but I'll have to. This isn't going to end here."

Vickie refused to give in. "You'll have to get me in there first. I'll make enough noise that somebody will say something."

"In this neighborhood? I doubt it."

Upstairs, Alexis slipped through the window one more time. However, as she dropped in, the ax slipped out of her hands. It made a loud clunk on the floor, which echoed throughout the empty house.

Jim looked at Vickie with his eyebrows raised. "What was that?"

Vickie shrugged. "There are people who know we're here. I won't be surprised if somebody just walked into the house."

He grabbed the sword at his side and raised it. "Well, they're not going to be here long."

CHAPTER TWENTY-SEVEN

Vickie held tightly to the handcuff attached to her left hand. She couldn't sense who was in the house. She didn't know if it was a friend or a foe.

I'm nervous, and I can't see anything! Is this what it's like to be human all the time? How does one go through life not being able to see what's going on around them? Who's there?

Jim paced, bouncing on his heels as he clung to the sword. "Go ahead!" he shouted. "Come on down already! You've already blown your surprise, so let's just go!"

The basement steps creaked loudly as Alexis walked down them. Her hands shook, but she held the ax high, ready to swing it if needed. Once her feet were visible, Vickie's stomach dropped.

"Alexis!" Her voice held a mix of relief and sadness. Relief that it was her friend, and sadness because she was endangering herself.

Jim laughed when he saw her. "Oh, it's just you."

Alexis mustered whatever bravery she could, but her voice wavered as she spoke. "Let her go. Now."

"Or what?" He let out another belly laugh and spoke in a mocking tone. "You're going to chop me down with that ax? Sweetheart, there was a reason I left it there. I'm not worried about you having it. You want to take a swing? Do it. Go on, I'll give you the first shot." He extended his arms and stuck his chin out, taunting her.

"Don't do it, Alexis." Vickie shook her head, watching intently.

"I'm not going to." Alexis squeezed the ax handle. "As long as you let her go, I'll let you live."

Jim closed his eyes and chuckled. "Which movie did you lift that from? You sound like a bad script. Listen, honey, I don't want to hurt you, okay? You didn't do anything to me. And honestly, I'm not going to hurt your friend here, either. She's just going to come with me. We're getting out of here, and you're going to get out of our way."

Alexis shook her head nervously. "No, I'm not."

"This is adorable, but we're reaching the end. I don't have time to play any more games. Step aside, go home, do whatever you want, but this vampire is coming with me."

She pressed her lips together. "What if I don't?"

"Seriously? Child, I will stop at nothing to keep this creature. If you get in the way, I might have to react violently, and I will tell you right now, a grown man with a sword will beat a little girl with an ax every time."

"She's not a creature. She's my sister. I've already lost one family member. I'm not letting another one go."

Vickie was touched by the sentiment, but she couldn't allow herself to be moved by it. She was still terrified that Jim would hurt Alexis. *If he touches one hair on her head, I'm going to go crazy. He won't be able to restrain me. I don't care about the sword.*

"You're right," Alexis said. "I won't beat you with an ax." She dropped it to the floor.

"Alexis, what are you doing? Are you nuts?" Vickie shouted.

Her friend reached into her waistband and pulled out a gun, pointing it at Jim. "I brought a gun to a sword fight. Isn't that how it goes?"

Jim froze. "That's not how it goes, but well done. You win. I'm going to put the sword down." Without thinking, Jim dropped the sword, and it fell behind him, just in front of Vickie.

"Thank you." Alexis' confidence grew. "Now, unlock those handcuffs and let her go."

With his hands in the air, Jim nodded. "Okay. I'll move slowly. Just let me..." He spun with a gun of his own, pointing it at Vickie's head. "Now, you'll put down *your* gun, or I'll just shoot her right now and this will all be over —and it'll be your fault."

Alexis raised her free hand to stop him. "Wait. Don't. Please. Don't hurt her. I'll put it down."

"Don't do it, Alexis!" Vickie shouted at her. She didn't appear concerned about the barrel of the gun digging into the side of her head.

"I don't want him to shoot you! I'm here to help, not kill you!"

"He's not going to shoot me. He can't." She rolled her eyes. "You are obsessed with getting me to Washington and putting me at the feet of the government. How would killing me help that? You don't want me dead. You're just acting impulsively and hoping you can scare her into disarming herself. Alexis, you hang onto that gun!"

Jim shook his head. "Fine. You're right, I'm not going to shoot her. I'll shoot you instead." He turned the barrel to point it at Alexis and let Vickie go, moving out of her reach once again. "You're all heroic, but you're just going to die for your trouble, and your friend here—sorry, your *sister*—is going to watch it happen in front of her. All you've done is make everything worse."

"What if I shoot you first? I have a gun, too."

Jim gave her a devilish smile. "Is it loaded?"

Alexis' expression fell. She looked at the gun in her hands, then back at Jim. "Yes."

"Are you sure about that? I'm starting to think that it's not."

"Why would you think it's not loaded?"

He shrugged. "Your dad is responsible enough to keep the gun in a gun safe under lock and key. He's probably also responsible enough to not keep it loaded. So if you just grabbed the gun and ran off without loading it, there's probably not one bullet in that chamber."

Alexis shook her head. "I bet there is."

"Prove it."

"What?"

"Prove it. Pull the trigger right now. Shoot me. I bet you'll hear a click and nothing will happen." He lowered his eyes. "But if you do pull the trigger and nothing happens, it's not going to end well for you."

Vickie's mouth hung open. "You wouldn't."

"Yeah, I really would. I don't want to, but I would. I'm tired of playing games with you girls. I have fourteen hours of driving ahead of me, and I want to hit the road. So, this is what you can do, girl. Try to shoot me and see what happens next, or you can quietly walk back up those stairs and out the door. The choice is yours."

"Alexis…" Vickie began, her voice choking up. "Just go. I can take care of myself. Really."

"No! I'm not leaving here without you."

"If he shoots you, you're not leaving here at all! He's won. I have to go with him."

Jim nodded at Vickie. "Smart girl. You'd be wise to listen to her. I'm not a bad guy. I'm just a man who is trying to do his job, and if you get in the way of that, I have to get you out of the way. I'm not going to shoot you for no reason. That would be cold. But if you try to kill me, I'm going to defend myself. Either way, I'm leaving with the vampire."

The two girls remained silent. All Vickie wanted was for Alexis to leave and save herself, but the thought would not cross Alexis' mind. From her perspective, she was staring at her own death, rather than abandoning Vickie.

"Think about it," Jim continued. "You go home, start fixing up your house, get a new front door. You go back to your normal life. No vampires around to add to the drama or the danger of your life anymore. You get a nice, normal summer vacation free from supernatural responsibilities. Or, you stay here, try to be a hero, and die in the disgusting basement of a random, rotting house on the north side of Milwaukee. Is that what you want? It's not what I want. I want to let you go."

"Come on, Alexis. Just go. Please. Don't do this."

Alexis looked at Vickie somberly, then slowly lowered her gun.

"Atta girl." Jim nodded, relieved. "You made a smart choice. Now nobody has to get hurt."

In a flash, Alexis raised the gun again and pulled the trigger, but to her terror, the gun indeed did click, but no bullet emerged. When she realized this, she closed her eyes and hung her head.

Jim sighed. "I told you to go. I tried to get you to go. I gave you every chance in the world to leave with your head held high. It didn't have to be this way."

"Alexis!" Vickie gasped.

As she watched Jim aiming the gun at her, rage built inside of Vickie. *The family bond. I'm her family. That connection is stronger than anything, even my vampire powers.*

Jim pulled back the hammer on his gun, and the *click* echoed through the empty basement. "You need to understand that this gives me no joy at all. I don't want to do this, but I have to bring this girl to Washington, whether you like it or not. You chose this fate. All I'm doing is living up to my word."

Alexis craned her neck, gritting her teeth as she began to sob involuntarily. "I really thought it was loaded," she whispered.

"Obviously." Jim looked at her glumly. "For your sake, I wish it had been. But now, I have to do what I set out to do, and that's get the vampire out of here. I'm sorry."

He placed his finger on the trigger.

CHAPTER TWENTY-EIGHT

*V*ickie, *whatever you have inside yourself right now, use it. NOW.*

The powerless vampire girl scanned the area and saw the sword just within reach. Moving as quickly as she could, Vickie lunged for the sword, digging the handcuff into her wrist so hard she broke the skin. She groaned in pain but reached the hilt. With a surge of adrenaline, she hoisted the heavy weapon off the ground with her right hand and flung it like a dart at Jim Trembo.

The sword floated in the air and the tip lodged in his thigh, just below his hip. The weight of the handle pulled the sword down, tearing open a gaping wound.

Jim screamed in pain and collapsed to the floor, dropping his gun. It was just out of reach for Vickie, who dove for it. Her fingertips barely touched the butt.

Trembo saw her reaching for it and tried to crawl over and grab it. Thinking quickly, Alexis charged in and kicked the gun away from him and toward Vickie. Because of where she was standing, he grabbed her leg instead, trying desperately to regain control of the situation.

Vickie moved quickly, using a set of survival instincts she didn't know she had. She picked up the gun and fired a shot at Jim, striking him in the shoulder and knocking him onto the floor. Alexis broke free of his grip and ran toward the stairs.

With blood running down her arm and her leg wound torn open again amidst the chaos, Vickie looked like the victim in a horror movie. However, she wore a look of confidence as she stared down the barrel of the gun at Jim Trembo.

He stretched out his hand and shook his head. "Please don't. I wasn't going to shoot her. Seriously."

Sirens blared in the distance, and they were growing louder. "You're in a lot of trouble right now, Jim." Vickie smiled. "Toss her the key to these handcuffs—and move slowly. If you make one false move, I'll shoot."

"Okay, okay." He grunted as he rolled onto his side to free his right hand. He pulled a set of keys out of his pocket and weakly tossed them to Alexis.

"Come get me out of here. I need to get rid of something before the cops get here."

Confused, Alexis picked up the keys, ran over to Vickie, and unlocked the handcuffs. She moaned in relief as her hand fell. "Oh, my goodness, that hurt. Okay, take the gun."

"Me? Really?"

"Yeah. You showed me you're not afraid to pull the trigger when you need to. Just keep it pointed at him."

She took the gun from Vickie. "What are you going to do?"

"I need to get rid of this thing for now." Vickie picked up the sword by the hilt, dragging the blade over the concrete. She limped on her good leg.

"Are you sure you don't want me to do something with it? Why don't you just leave it here?"

Vickie stopped at the base of the stairs. "No. I want this stupid thing to be my responsibility, and if I leave it here, it gives him ammo. If it's nowhere to be found, then he's insane. Trust me."

Alexis didn't understand what Vickie was trying to tell her, but she did what she was told. She leaned against the pipe and kept both hands on the gun, staring at Jim Trembo while Vickie lugged the sword up the stairs. "You were going to shoot a defenseless teenage girl." She shook her head in disgust. "You should be ashamed of yourself."

Jim rested his head on the concrete, taking deep breaths to keep his body from going into shock as he stared at the ceiling. "I'm not proud of it."

"You shouldn't be. And you know what's even better?"

"What?"

"You tried to shoot a defenseless teenage girl…and you lost the fight."

At the top of the stairs, Vickie propped the sword against her body while she fiddled with the lock on the back door. Eventually, she pulled the door open and dragged the weapon out into the backyard.

The sirens were getting closer. *I don't have a lot of time. I have to put this thing somewhere it won't be found but I can get to it later.* She lugged the sword across the backyard to the garage. To her delight, the side door was open. Peeking in, she confirmed nobody was inside, so she dragged the sword to the front, near the garage door.

Vickie tucked the sword into the corner. *Hopefully nobody comes out here to snoop around. I can come get it tomorrow. Now, to just get as far from this thing as I can right now.*

By the time she reached the house, the lights of the police cars were rushing down the street. She hurried back in and locked the door, descending the stairs to return to the scene of the crime.

In the basement, she took a deep breath and smiled. Her face lit up, and Alexis looked at her in surprise. "You okay?"

"Yes. Yes, I am." Vickie had gotten far enough away from the sword that her powers had returned. An overwhelming sense of comfort washed over her; she once again felt in control of her body. "I'm a vampire again."

Alexis nodded. "Are you going to heal those two wounds, then?"

She shook her head. "Not yet. I'm not going to give him anything that would support his argument." She looked at Jim, who was shivering on the concrete, his body going into shock. She limped over next to him and looked down at him in disgust. "The police are here. They'll get you fixed up, and then they'll arrest you for kidnapping a minor."

"I-I…" He gritted his teeth, trying to keep them from chattering. "I was just trying to do my job."

Vickie shook her head. "Doesn't matter now. All that matters is you'll be arrested, and you won't have a job anymore."

"I don't have a job *now*. You were here for it all. They've abandoned me. You have all the freedom you could want."

The vampire placed her hand on her stomach and looked at Alexis. "You know what?"

"What?"

"I feel great right now. Best I've felt in months."

Alexis smiled. "Good for you. I guess that means we've got the right guy."

Vickie looked at the gunshot wound in Trembo's shoulder. "I would have figured a gunshot would have attracted attention around here. I mean, this *is* a residential neighborhood."

"Not *this* neighborhood. We're used to gunshots. Doesn't make an impact. What did you do with the sword?"

"I tucked it away. I don't want the police to find out about it. They'll start sniffing around, and I'll be outed anyway. I want Jim here to look as insane as possible."

Alexis nodded. "A good plan." She tilted her head, looking at Jim's leg. "But what about the other wound? How do we explain that one?"

Vickie put her hands on her hips. Alexis was right; the sword had cut his leg. She snapped her fingers. She bent over and picked up the ax, bringing it to Jim's side. "I'm not doing this to make it hurt any more than it already does," she assured him. "I'm just covering our tracks."

He wailed in pain as she lightly dug the blade of the ax into his leg. Alexis winced. "Ugh."

"That's plenty." Vickie pulled the ax out and left it lying by his side. "There. Now it looks like the ax did the damage, not the sword."

The vampire walked over to the pipe and sat down next to Alexis, shoulder to shoulder. She put her head on Alexis' shoulder, and Alexis tilted her head to rest on Vickie's. "Thanks for standing up for me."

Alexis smiled, keeping the gun aimed at Jim, who was in no condition to retaliate anyway. "That's what family does. We look out for each other. We put it on the line for each other, you know?"

"Yeah, I do know that. My parents taught me a long time ago that the bond of family was stronger than any superpower a vampire has."

"Sounds like they were smart people, Vickie."

"They were, and they taught me well. Tonight just proved it. Are you okay? How do you feel?"

Alexis tilted her head back and forth. "I'm a little shaken up. Also freaked out. I think I'll sleep for a week and a half after this."

Vickie laughed. "I feel like I'm going to sleep for a month when we get out of here."

They heard pounding on the front door and a distant voice. "THIS IS THE POLICE!"

Vickie pulled herself to her feet and limped to the stairs to scream, "We're down in the basement!"

The police officers knocked down the front door and rushed in. Waiting outside, Craig, Eric, and Charlie stood on the sidewalk, holding their breath and hoping the girls were okay.

"I heard Vickie!" Eric announced.

"I just hope that means Alexis is okay, too," Charlie commented.

Craig threw his arm around Charlie's shoulder. "Me, too, son. I'm sure she is." He wasn't sure, but Craig wasn't about to entertain the thought that he had lost his entire family inside of one calendar year.

He held his breath. *If something happened to either of them while I was out on a date, I'd never forgive myself.*

CHAPTER TWENTY-NINE

With their guns drawn, the officers charged into the house and down the basement steps. "Geez!" one of them yelled upon seeing the bloody scene.

One officer ran over to Jim Trembo and grabbed his wrist, checking his pulse. He pushed a button on the radio attached to his shoulder. "We've got one man down with multiple wounds, and a female with injuries. Let's get some paramedics down here to tend to them both."

"You girls okay?" one officer said as he approached. "I'm Officer Jacobson, and that's my partner, Officer Diaz." He pushed the button on his radio. "Area is secured. Both victims appear to be safe and in good health, despite some injuries."

One of the officers outside turned to Craig and the boys as paramedics rushed into the house. "We've got word that both girls are okay. Just hang on for a few minutes, and we'll get them out of there."

Eric and Charlie both exhaled deeply, hugging each

other in celebration. Craig, meanwhile, broke down into tears upon hearing the news.

"You okay, Mr. Watson?"

He swallowed hard. "Yeah. I'm okay now."

In the basement, the officers were asking the girls about what had happened. Vickie took the lead. "He broke into our house and dragged me away. You'll see blood on the sidewalk between our house and this one, and the front door was destroyed. He never explained why he was doing it."

"Did he do anything to you?" Diaz asked as delicately as he could while observing the handcuffs dangling from the pipe.

"He just brought me down here and handcuffed me. He didn't touch me or anything like that."

Jacobson was taking notes. "He didn't talk about why he was doing this? He just brought you here and restrained you?"

Vickie shrugged. "Basically, yeah. He didn't beat me. He didn't do anything inappropriate. I don't know if he was planning to, but she showed up and threw off his game plan."

"And what did you do?" Diaz looked at Alexis.

"Oh, um… I, uh…he brought the ax to our house and left it there. So I brought it with me and followed the blood here. I was trying to help."

"Why didn't you call the police instead of trying to be the hero?" Diaz asked.

Vickie jumped in, knowing Alexis couldn't answer that truthfully. "I think we all were in shock. When you get to the house, you'll see what I mean. He chopped his way in. It was very scary. We were just running on instinct. That's kinda how we got out of it, in all honesty." She explained how they had attacked him and freed themselves.

The paramedics had already strapped Jim to a stretcher and were tending to his wounds. Jacobson walked over to him as they lifted the stretcher off the ground. "Get well soon, buddy, because you're going to have to answer a whole lot of questions about this!"

Diaz handed him Trembo's wallet. "Check it out. He's a fed."

Jacobson grabbed the wallet and inspected his ID. "Holy cow, he is. What the heck is a federal agent doing kidnapping teenage girls?" He rubbed his temples. "This is going to be one complicated case to get through."

The paramedics wrapped Vickie's leg, finally stopping the bleeding, and they bandaged her wrist as well.

Jacobson reviewed his notes. "So you never met this guy before. You didn't let him into your house. He kidnapped you, dragging you to this place for no apparent reason."

Vickie shrugged. "That sounds about right. I mean, we had seen him at our high school. We were told he was some kind of special hall monitor. I don't think anyone knew what was going on with that, but we recognized him from there."

Jacobson and Diaz exchanged confused looks.

Diaz shook his head in disbelief. "Did this guy use his federal credentials to get access to high school girls? Do you two know of any other girls who have had run-ins with this guy?"

"Not that we know of." Alexis crossed her arms. "Maybe we were his first victims."

"We'll look into it," Jacobson said. "Some fellas are outside, waiting for you both. I think we have enough information for now. Let's get you out there and back to where you belong."

When the girls stumbled out the front door, news crews had already assembled on the street, blocking the flow of traffic. Once they descended the wooden steps, Craig sprinted up to them and wrapped them both in his arms.

"Thank God, thank God, thank God…" he repeated over and over. "I'm so happy you two are okay. So, so happy. You *are* okay, right? Tell me you're okay. What did he do to you?"

The girls held him tightly as Alexis explained, "We're okay, Dad. Really. He didn't do anything to us. Just gave us a good scare, that's all."

He let them go so the boys could greet them and hug them. Exhausted, Vickie sat down on the concrete steps in front of the house. Craig sat next to her.

"Please tell me this was the horrible thing you have been sensing for weeks. I don't think I could survive anything else this dramatic."

Vickie laughed and nodded. "I think so. All my powers are back, and they feel fine. I think it's over now. Well, almost."

"Almost?"

She looked around to make sure nobody was watching or listening. "I stashed something. We have to come back here tomorrow to get it, and we'll have to figure out what to do with it. I want it destroyed so nobody can wield it ever again."

"Gotcha. You look a little worse for wear. Are you able to fix yourself up?"

"Definitely, but I wanted to wait until everything died down. Once they're done looking at me and we're at home, I'll heal."

They stood up to see Trembo being carted off on a stretcher, a bag of blood being pumped into his system to keep him alive. Craig walked up to him, but the officers cut him off.

"I just want to see who laid his hands on my girls."

"I know, sir," Jacobson said. "I get it. But we need to make sure he gets to the hospital and is fixed up so he can stand trial for his crimes. You'll see him in court."

Rage burned inside Craig, but he relented, catching a glimpse of him as he was being loaded into the ambulance. "I think I've talked to him before. He was at my door months ago."

Diaz shook his head as Craig explained it to him. "This guy ran one long con. I wonder if he's really a federal agent!"

Craig shuffled back to his daughter and hugged her again. "He didn't do anything to you?"

"No. I was going to kill *him*, but somebody didn't load his gun!"

He laughed. "You mean to tell me that my little girl tried to shoot a dangerous criminal with my gun?"

Vickie joined them. "Yep. I was helpless, and your daughter stepped up. She confronted him and didn't back down, even when I begged her to. You should be proud of her."

"I am *very* proud of her." He held Alexis tight and kissed the top of her head. "Very, very proud. And relieved."

Vickie pulled Eric aside and nodded to Charlie. "What does he know?"

"Charlie? Nothing. He knows as much as the police do."

"No vampire stuff?"

"Nope. I kept my mouth shut." He wrapped his arms around his girlfriend. "Is this how it's going to be, dating a vampire? Should I expect this to happen every few months? Once a year? What?"

She buried her face in his shoulder. "I sure hope not. No, this is the worst it's going to be, and we're taking steps to make sure it never happens again."

Later that night, Vickie stood in the bathroom, inspecting the cuts, wounds, and bruises on her body. She held onto the countertop, closed her eyes, and began breathing deeply, sending her powers into overdrive once again. One by one, her wounds closed, her bruises disappeared, and her body was restored to perfect health. She opened her eyes and smiled into the mirror.

"I've missed you."

The next morning, Craig took Vickie to the alley behind the house on 53rd Street in the SUV. They parked right behind it, in front of the garage.

"Is this good?"

"Yep. I can already feel my powers disappearing." She jumped out of the vehicle, slipped into the garage, and emerged with the sword. Vickie quickly opened the back door, tossed the sword in, and closed it. She climbed back into the car and said, "Okay, drive."

"I've already called my friend Barry," Craig said as they drove to the dump. "He works in waste management. I told him I needed something taken care of. He said he trusted that I wasn't going to be breaking any laws and that he wouldn't have it pinned on him."

"Perfect."

They pulled into the parking lot of the dump, which was closed on Sunday, and he waved at a middle-aged man with a bushy mustache who came out to greet them.

"Hey, Craig!" He shook his hand.

"Barry. Ready to do this?"

"Sure, just pull on through."

Moments later, they got out of the SUV and pulled the sword out of the back seat.

Barry gave them a concerned look. "This isn't a murder weapon, is it?"

"No." Vickie met his gaze. "In fact, we're doing this to *prevent* it from ever being a murder weapon."

"Okay. I trust you. Craig's a good guy. He wouldn't do anything." He took it from Vickie's hands and whistled. "This is a beautiful thing. You really ought to clean it up. I bet there's history there. Would make a great conversation piece."

"Yeah, but it could end up in the wrong hands, Barry. That's why we're here. And if you don't mind, we'd like to watch it go into the incinerator, so we don't ever have to question whether it's…well, *anywhere*."

"Got it. Follow me."

They walked into the waste management facility, which

was silent because none of the equipment was running. Barry flipped a switch at the far end of the warehouse, which resulted in a loud hum.

"She's just warming up. Give it a second. I'll even let you throw it in if you want."

Vickie cocked an eyebrow. "Seriously? Yes, let's do that."

"You got it." A few minutes later, he slipped on a glove and pulled a lever, opening a door that let out a blast of heat. "Try not to get too close. Just toss it in there, and we'll take care of the rest."

Vickie looked at the sword and its ornate hilt. The weapon had nearly killed her twice. The weapon had cut down the vampire race and killed her family.

She closed her eyes and held it close. *Mutter. Vater. Today, I lay to rest the evil that stole the lives of both of you and my siblings. The world is finally free of the scourge of the Circle.*

With that, she threw the sword into the incinerator. Barry closed the door and flipped another switch, turning the heat up to high.

"Give me a moment." Vickie held up a finger, standing next to the incinerator as it did its job. Craig watched her carefully. Finally, she opened her eyes and looked at him, nodding. "It's done."

They thanked Barry and got back into the SUV. Craig clipped his seatbelt and glanced at her. "So, you're a vampire again? Full-force?"

Vickie nodded, gazing at the facility where the sword had been destroyed. "Now and forever."

CHAPTER THIRTY

Alexis poked her head into Vickie's room. "Hey, Vickie, the boys are going to be here soon. You said you were cleaning up."

"I know, I know." Vickie got up off her bed and walked across the house to the front closet, where the vacuum was stored. She pulled it out as Alexis headed back into the kitchen to finish washing the dishes.

Craig picked up the remote and paused the local news. "Going to vacuum?"

"Yep. I thought you hated the news."

"I do, but they're going to be talking about your case. I figured we could have a good laugh over the whole thing. I'll just keep it paused. Hurry up, though, okay?" He winked at her.

"Okay. I'll try." After plugging in the vacuum, Vickie closed her eyes and took a few deep breaths, activating the powers inside her. In a flash, she vacuumed the entire house, bouncing from room to room and returning to the living room a few seconds later. "Clean."

"Thanks. I hope you don't mind using your powers like that."

Vickie shrugged. "As long as I'm not the only one cleaning around here, I don't care."

Alexis called from the kitchen, "Hey, come finish these dishes so I can sit on the couch."

"Yeah, right!"

"Actually, Lex, come in here! They're going to talk about Trembo!"

"Oooh!" Alexis tossed the dishtowel on the open dishwasher rack and ran into the living room to join them as Vickie was shoving the vacuum cleaner back in the closet. "This ought to be good."

Craig turned it up as the reporter began to speak.

Tonight's top story: one of the city's most disturbing criminals is brought to justice. James Trembo, a man who claimed to be a federal agent in charge of investigating high school students, was sentenced today to forty years in prison for kidnapping and inflicting injury on a fourteen-year-old girl, dragging her from her home and holding her hostage in an abandoned house two blocks away. Trembo claimed he was employed by a secret federal agency in charge of investigating supernatural activity, and he was led to Milwaukee to research the existence of vampires. Police say he claimed the girl he kidnapped was a vampire, and he was going to take her to Washington for research purposes. Sources spoke to a number of federal agents, including Doug Casey, the head of the Department of Homeland Security, and they all deny both the existence of a supernatural department of the federal government and the credentials of James Trembo. Federal representatives told us there is no record of Trembo ever working in Wash-

*ington and that he is clearly suffering from some sort of
delusion.*

"This may be the funniest thing to ever happen in my
life," Craig said. "And you say he was on the phone with
agents and stuff?"

"He was clearly working for them, but he lost his mind
because they were all ditching him. They didn't believe
him. I knew that as long as I removed the sword from the
premises, he had no proof that could possibly connect him
to vampires or anything. And based on how his conversations with his bosses went, they were all going to ditch him
instead of vouch for him."

"That's the US government for ya."

What the family did not know was that everyone in Jim
Trembo's department, including Pete Stabone, had been
reassigned to other areas, and the department was shut
down for good. In an effort to avoid a PR disaster, they
wiped away any evidence of its existence and moved on
with their lives, forgetting that Jim Trembo had ever
worked for them.

The doorbell rang, and Alexis greeted Charlie at the
door. He walked in and said hello to everyone.

"I just heard that the Trembo guy got sentenced today.
What a maniac. He thought you were a vampire? Guy's got
a few screws loose!" He laughed. "At least it's good to laugh
about it before anything terrible actually happened, am I
right?"

They nodded. Alexis took him by the hand, and they sat
on the couch. "Pizza will be ready soon."

Craig lowered the footrest on the chair and stood up. "I
suppose I should be getting ready too." He walked down

the hall to his room, where he changed his shirt. Before leaving the room, he grabbed the key from his dresser and crouched next to the bed.

He pulled out his gun safe and unlocked it to double-check the weapon. *Locked and loaded. Good.*

After locking it again and heading to the bathroom, he combed his hair and splashed on some cologne. Vickie came up to him. "Big night tonight."

"Yeah! Going to be a really nice dinner."

"I'm so glad Katie didn't get mad at you for ditching out on your date that night. I felt bad."

He screwed the cap onto his cologne and looked at her seriously. "Listen, if she'd decided I wasn't worth dating because I had to take care of a serious situation involving my girls, I would have stopped dating her anyway. She wouldn't have been worth it. But she's a sweetheart, and things have been awesome since." He looked in the mirror. "How do I look?"

"Like a million bucks." Vickie patted him on the back.

"Are you sure you're going to be all right tonight? I mean, the last time we tried to do this…"

"My stomach is rock solid, and my powers are at full force. Nothing is going to happen, I assure you. Go have fun, and don't worry about us one bit. Besides, the guys will be here, too. Nobody's going to mess with us."

He sighed. "I hope those aren't famous last words."

Vickie jogged to the front door upon hearing the doorbell, and she let Eric in. He greeted her with a kiss. "Let's try this again, shall we?"

She laughed. "I know. Craig is really worried that this is going to happen again."

"How are you feeling?"

"Great. This is going to be the exact opposite of that night."

Craig slipped on his shoes and grabbed his keys. He stopped in the living room before heading out. "You guys behave. Boys, I'm watching you both. Hey, Lex? Come here for a sec."

Alexis joined him in the kitchen. "What's up, Dad?"

"Just so you know, the gun is loaded this time." He gave her a smile.

"Dad, everything will be fine. You've got nothing to worry about."

"I know. But I'm always going to worry. You know that."

"Go have fun tonight. Maybe next time, Katie can come here, and we can meet her."

"If things go well tonight, she *will* be coming here. Be safe. I love you."

"I love you too, Dad." She gave him a hug and returned to the living room.

Craig walked out, started the SUV, and backed out of the driveway. Before he took off, he took one more look at the brand-new reinforced front door, then sped off to meet Katie for dinner.

In the living room, the two couples curled up on the couch, eating pizza and watching a movie. As they enjoyed themselves, a sense of calm and peace washed over Vickie.

I spent four hundred years in complete silence, and this is the most peaceful and calm I've ever felt in my life. Maybe getting out of there wasn't a mistake after all. I'm right where I'm supposed to be now.

She leaned into Eric, who wrapped his arm around her and held her tight while a calm summer breeze blew through the window.

THE END

This story might be ending, but we have many more to tell. Keep an eye out for new series releasing in the coming year, including: The Adventures of Finnegan Dragonbender, The Witches of Pressler Street, Scions of Magic, Dwarf Bounty Hunter and more.

Get sneak peeks, exclusive giveaways, behind the scenes content, and more.
PLUS you'll be notified of special **one day only fan pricing** on new releases.

Sign up today to get free stories.

CLICK HERE

or visit: https://marthacarr.com/read-free-stories/

AUTHOR NOTES - MARTHA CARR

NOVEMBER 26, 2019

It's a dog eat dog world out there and I'm wearing milk-bone shorts. This is the everything dog news edition with some catching up to do.

If you could see where I'm sitting, you'd wonder why someone would work so hard to buy their dreamhouse with a grand office and a cool Warhol-esque portrait of Yumfuck Tiberius Troll and a big desk with a very tall window that looks out onto tall trees– and they're sitting in their kitchen typing.

Enter the good dog, Lois Lane and her sidekick, the sweet pittie, Leela. They have protected the house from every neighbor, random deer, our first squirrel sighting, delivery trucks and tree branches blowing in the breeze – with loud, continual barking. Lois' bark sounds like she's shouting, "Drop the drugs!" And it's the only volume she has. There's no modulation, no variance in pitch. This one type of loud, deep, feel it in your chest bark.

Imagine being deep in thought, about to throw a fire-ball at some bad guy or even better, melting them with a red tide that's seeping up to their shoes. And, just when I'm at the good part, I've forgotten where I am, the words are rolling – Lois lets out a fierce, low and very loud bark. It restarts my heart every time.

Lois was also born deaf – she knows hand signals and does great – and is a very smart dog. When she doesn't want to see me doing the signal for *Stop That* – she turns away or rolls her eyes to the ceiling. I tried everything to get her to stop. Behavior modification, treats, stern looks, shutting her out of the office. Nothing really worked. Instead, she was teaching Leela how to join in on the chorus.

So here I am, sitting in the kitchen. It's a really nice kitchen. This is a high-class problem.

The sweet Pittie, Leela used to be the Offspring's dog till living arrangements got shuffled and Leela needed a place to land. She was originally used and abused by dog fighters and then dumped on the street – and still has the most soulful eyes with the sweetest disposition. But she's also generally anxious, watching humans to see if they're okay, even tempered, easy to get along with. She may never lose that. So, I took her in to give her stability, someone she kind of knows and to spoil her till the end of her days. She already has a graying muzzle and last year, just after I got her, we fixed one of her back knees. I turned 60 this year, Leela, I feel ya.

Lately, she's been feeling her oats, chasing after Lois who outweighs her by thirty pounds. Lois is a big girl. Leela has tried to run full force into Lois a couple of times, only to bounce off her like she hit a trampoline. Doesn't stop her from giving it another go occasionally. I like that can-do spirit. She's a little indie dog in an indie household.

The latest big news though is that the Offspring has adopted another dog… A porgie – part pittie, part corgie that he's named Dude and is calling, Little Dude. Pale cream color with white markings who is reported to be 'very chill'. He joined the Offspring's last week and will be introduced to Lois and Leela at some point, but for now I'm getting a lot of photos and videos. No, I'm not mentioning the obvious about Leela over here. She was probably moved around enough and needed a home that she knew would be hers for the rest of her days. Even one with a grand office that they sit in and some strange lady sitting in the kitchen leaning over a computer, typing away. (Except for when she gets up to hand out treats or run around the backyard with them.) More adventures to follow.

Thank you for not only reading this story, but these author notes as well!

I have officially just had my first Thanksgiving without our children at home. All three of them are presently living in Texas while Judith and I are in Texas at the moment enjoying Thanksgiving with my older brother and his spouse, Carlos.

We had a delicious Thanksgiving dinner prepared well in advance at the nice bistro in his community.

All of the Turkey, mashed potatoes, rolls etc. I could possibly want and none of the cleaning up to worry about. While I missed the boys, I'm not sure I miss the mess and effort of helping (even just *helping*) cook the large meal and all of the preparation that goes with a Thanksgiving dinner.

It was nice to get together with them as I doubt I'll see them again until perhaps late May of 2020. Perhaps. If we miss that opportunity it might be at our 10th Anniversary in June.

Now that Thanksgiving is finished, we look forward to flying to Dallas near Christmas for a chance to see one of the boys (Joseph) and have let Joshua and Jacob know we will be up there in case they can make it.

Not sure they will, actually.

It's a little hard to handle the whole empty nest syndrome. Which is a little strange as I was so looking forward to HAVING an empty nest. I'm proud of our guys, and eventually they might have families of their own and Thanksgiving and Christmas needs to be about their personal families so time together will be less and less.

Judith and I travel, a lot, for this publishing company (LMBPN). We hit multiple countries in a year and by the time I get back I just want to pull my arms and legs in like a turtle and hide from the world.

From the very beginning of my author career I showed Jacob and Joseph (the twins) everything I was doing. They were sophomores in high school, and while they didn't understand at the time, I hope that as they grow older that the experience of seeing the effort (and the success) might provide encouragement that they can make their dreams come true.

Or at least hard work and a bit of luck pays off?

Either way – as we drive up the 34 towards our home, I hope they are enjoying their life as they spread their wings and fly.

I hope your future is bright, and if you have children at home just know that they actually do leave (well, most of them) and it can be a bit melancholic at times. But, life doesn't move forward if they don't.

Ad Aeternitatem,

Michael

Series in the Oriceran Universe:

SCHOOL OF NECESSARY MAGIC
SCHOOL OF NECESSARY MAGIC: RAINE CAMPBELL
ALISON BROWNSTONE
THE DANIEL CODEX SERIES
THE LEIRA CHRONICLES
I FEAR NO EVIL
FEDERAL AGENTS OF MAGIC
THE UNBELIEVABLE MR. BROWNSTONE
REWRITING JUSTICE
THE KACY CHRONICLES
MIDWEST MAGIC CHRONICLES
SOUL STONE MAGE
THE FAIRHAVEN CHRONICLES

Other series:

THE LAST VAMPIRE

THE WITCH NEXT DOOR

OTHER BOOKS BY JUDITH BERENS

OTHER BOOKS BY MARTHA CARR

JOIN THE ORICERAN UNIVERSE FAN GROUP ON FACEBOOK!